Wolfgang Koeppen was born in 1906 and died ninety years later in Munich. He published five novels, two in the 1930s and three in the 1950s. In 1962 he won the Büchner Prize, Germany's most prestigious literary award. He is being posthumously recognized as a giant of European literature.

Michael Hofmann is a poet. He is the translator of eight books by Joseph Roth and was awarded the PEN/Book-of-the-Month Club Prize for translating *The String of Pearls* (Granta Books).

A Sad Affair

WOLFGANG KOEPPEN

TRANSLATED WITH AN INTRODUCTION BY

MICHAEL HOFMANN

Granta Books
London

Granta Publications, 2/3 Hanover Yard, Noel Road, London N1 8BE

First published in Great Britain by Granta Books 2003
First published in the US by W. W. Norton & Company, Inc.
Originally published in German as *Eine unglückliche liebe*

Copyright © 1977 by Suhrkamp Verlag Frankfurt am Main
Introduction and translation copyright © 2003 by Michael Hofmann

A CIP catalogue record for this book
is available from the British Library.

1 3 5 7 9 10 8 6 4 2

Printed and bound in Great Britain
by Mackays of Chatham plc

INTRODUCTION

*T*HERE IS, obviously, a lot of literature about love, but a whole novel, and about one desperate, all-consuming, and unconsummated relationship, and little else besides?! One might come up with Goethe's *Sorrows of Young Werther*, Wedekind's *Lulu* plays, Heinrich Mann's *The Blue Angel*; there are a few similarities as well to Proust—Swann expending so much feeling on Odette, a woman who wasn't even his type, *"mon genre"*—and to Thomas Mann—Ingeborg Holm puts her hand, "not even a particularly slender or shapely little girl's hand," to the back of her head, and Tonio Kröger falls in love for a lifetime—but it remains true to say that the obsessive intensity of *A Sad Affair* is more like that of lyric poetry, painting, ballet, or song: Keats's "La Belle Dame sans Merci," Dowson's exquisite "Non sum qualis eram bonae sub regno

Cynarae," the pictures of Munch or Klimt or Schiele, *Swan Lake*, and any number of art songs and pop songs.

This is the more unexpected from an author who, in his masterly trilogy of novels from the 1950s—*Pigeons on the Grass* (1951), *The Hothouse* (1953), and *Death in Rome* (1954)—showed himself such an adept at the bigger picture: politics, history, society, culture. The world in those books, not unnaturally, is a fallen, a defeated, a recrudescent, and, in its bones, an unreformed world. It's as though the later Koeppen has turned on its head Pascal's nostrum about the cause of human misery being our inability to remain in our rooms; how, he argues, can there be anything as frail and contingent as human happiness, as long as the macro-scene is so full of iniquity? Surely everything—including our rooms and our selves—is warped, if not crushed, by the weight of these bigger tensions and untruths. Love is perhaps the most degraded thing of all: a feeling produced from cynicism, opportunism, or vacancy, a transaction somewhere on the scale between seduction and rape. In a world of rubble, where is one going to find a rose garden?

Koeppen said of himself—whereupon, helpfully, others said it of him—that he never wrote his books at the right time. Just as the books of the 1950s were published to howls of protest and indignation and hurt *amour-propre*, so this book he wrote in 1934—his debut, a young man's book—has nothing of Weimar or fascism or Germany. Its first action is to take its hero out of the country—never even named—and across a border. It barely deigns to use any place-names, and certainly no German ones: not until the action reaches Italy are streets and towns thought to be worth naming. Surely this already, this turning his back on the place just as it was so full of itself, so full of history and catastrophe, and on the cusp of much more history and catastrophe, is a gesture of tacit contempt. Nothing here for Left or Right, it seems to say: A curse on both your houses! Not that it has gone abroad to seek its political quarry either (as Koeppen did in *Death in Rome*, twenty years later); there is almost nothing of the feeling of gathering clouds, a restoration of national pride, and the sinister bombast of Mussolini (of the kind that Thomas Mann got into his wonderful short story from 1930, "Mario and the Magician"), no political curiosity at all. As we see from the later books, it wasn't that this type of thinking and writing was beyond Koeppen, even then, or ever. No, he wants to write the wrong book at the wrong time—even if it's his first.

It's hard to think of another writer as rebellious and ornery and uncompromising as Wolfgang Koeppen; I am reminded a little of Elizabeth Bishop, who said, "I have always written poetry more by not writing it." It was really not a time to make your debut with a love story, from a Jewish publisher. In a fine specimen of Nazi literary criticism—understood as an annex to the penal code, or, less formally, as an incitement to murder—one reviewer, Herbert Göpfert, fulminated:

I at any rate read nothing in these pages relating to love, only those surrogates that certain scribblers once offered in its place. The young persons in this squalid cabaret- and bordello-milieu, talking incessantly across each other of their repressed feelings, are such puny beings that one is forced to put the question quite directly: Are there really still such creatures among us, and if there are, do these striplings and tomboys have to be put in books? If it had been an old émigré writing like this, one might have understood—but a young poet, in our time? There's only one prescription I have to offer: labor camp!"

Koeppen, in Holland, managed to laugh. (*A Sad Affair* was duly put on the list of condemned books in 1936.)

What happened was this: Koeppen was a young journalist writing for the *Berliner Börsen-Courier*. A piece of his was seen and admired by Max Tau, an editor working for the prestigious Jewish publishing house of Bruno Cassirer. They met; Tau was very taken with Koeppen; offered him an advance to write a novel; Koeppen took the advance (took it to Italy), spent it, and came back without the novel. Max Tau—who does seem to have understood his man—realized that the carrot alone would not work, and offered a mild version of the stick to supplement it. They tried locking Koeppen up in empty apartments with a typewriter and plenty of paper. Eventually, one such arrangement worked, and Koeppen wrote his book—as I think he wrote all his books—very quickly. He had a resistance to writing, and in particular to writing what he thought someone else wanted or expected him to write, and this, in conjunction with his journalist's bad habit of leaving everything to the very last minute, must have made him an exasperating author. He wrote little in the course of a long career—five completed novels in sixty years—but when he did, the results were unexpected and worth having. The long periods of truancy surrounding short patches of zeal and productivity are a sort of guarantee. You don't get the oases without the desert. He was lucky in that he found three patient and supportive publishers, Cassirer, Henry Goverts, and latterly Suhrkamp. Tau said: "As an author, he was one of the compulsives, and encouragement and admonition weren't really much use. He would generally take off."

A *Sad Affair* (*Eine unglückliche Liebe*, but neither term translates well, and this is the only form of the pairing that I found satisfactory in English) is—it's no very great surprise—almost entirely true. (This also makes it an oddity in Koeppen's published fiction: elsewhere, he's not a straightforwardly autobiographical writer.) Friedrich seems utterly real: poor, vague, with secret, remote ambitions, educated, unworldly, intense, gauche, not perhaps very good at being young. The idea of him running everywhere is wonderful— a young man with a full heart and a full head, the sort of literary youth that probably went out of production in the 1980s. A little more surprising is the fact that Sibylle, the ideal and object—*subject* would be a better word—of Friedrich's passion is also about as real as a character in a book can be. She is based on Sibylle (*sic!*) Schloss, a young, half-Jewish (Koeppen doesn't say so) actress. When her career in the legitimate or serious theater was blocked as a result, she fell in with Erika Mann's anti-Fascist *Pfeffermühle* cabaret in Zurich (the unnamed foreign city of the novel), where the renowned German actress Therese Giehse also worked; Giehse, incidentally, is the somewhat Brechtian "peasant woman from olden days," and Mann herself is described as having "a Roman head." Koeppen (he doesn't say this either) wrote one or two chansons for his inamorata to perform. He persuaded her to visit Venice with him. Schloss was in her early twenties, heart-stoppingly beautiful, unconventional in her morality, and an interesting person with an interesting background (somewhat persiflaged by Koeppen). When it was published, Sibylle read and admired *Eine unglückliche Liebe*, and later on, when she worked in Brentano's bookshop on Fifth Avenue, she recommended the German edition to customers looking for "true-life romance." My source is a fascinating and very well-researched book called *Wolfgang Koeppen, 1933–1948*, published in 2001, by Jörg Döring, who tracked down and interviewed Sibylle Schloss on the Upper East Side, where she still lives. Other characters, like the wonderfully named Bosporus, Walter the critic, Fedor, and others, are also drawn from life. In fact, the only part of the book that is substantially made up is the adventure with Anja.

Tyranny has been described as the mother of metaphor, in which case, love—a state of emergency, a politics of two (a formulation that bridges the gap to Koeppen's later work)—perhaps might qualify as a form of tyranny. Certainly, it is a wonderfully generative—one might call it an aerobic—condition, fully exercising the image-making and likeness-building faculties of the imagination. Friedrich questions, rants, performs, devotes, hymns. He goes through all his gears, gets put through all his paces. And while he says "Yes," Sibylle as indefatigably and insistently says "No," perhaps the two great human freedoms. In her character, it seems to me, Koeppen investigates the pressure put upon beauty, a rather underexplored subject in fiction. Sibylle is a compassionately viewed victim, at least as much as she is a femme fatale, a Salome or a Jael or a Medusa. The beautiful are different, and not just because, as Hemingway would have had to have said, "They are better-looking." The accumulation of private expectation becomes almost a public pressure. The issue for beauty is how to be—or how not to be—publicly owned.

Still, *A Sad Affair* is mostly Friedrich's show, and the book is endearingly full of his instability, his zigs and zags, as he seeks forever to "travel," only to encounter the "frontiers" or the "glass wall" of another's being. (This is the principal metaphorical opposition in the book.) There are memorable descriptions of Friedrich and Sibylle as tunneling toward one another, of Friedrich as "the lover running amok," of Friedrich "in a desert in front of the cloud of a constant mirage." There are gorgeous poetic tributes to Sibylle, from the intimate but virginal "need to loiter in her breath and her bloodstream, to be a child in her womb" to the exalted yet delightfully playful "She was radiant, a contented snail in an invisible house of joy; a young kitten rolled into a ball, feeling the pleasure of being itself, and purring songs of praise to the Almighty," to the desperately sad and utterly authentic-sounding fallback, "She is my contemporary!" There is a lot of what I would call the "impossibilism" of the English Metaphysical love poets, Donne and Marvell, in Friedrich:

> My Love is of a birth as rare
> As 'tis for object strange and high:
> It was begotten by Despair
> Upon Impossibility.
>
> Magnanimous Despair alone
> Could show me so divine a thing,
> Where feeble Hope could ne'er have flown
> But vainly flapped its tinsel wing.
>
> —MARVELL, *"The Definition of Love"*

There are things that are too zany to be faked: Friedrich's superstitious game with himself in the lightbulb factory, nominating bulbs as characters in his drama, "At which point Sibylle went out"; the *folie à trois* with Beck, and the "days of the naughty Sibylles"; the serial, compulsory, rather demeaning friendships with the other men, Sibylle's successful lovers; the irritation with Magnus, not because he is a rival, but because, like himself, he is in love. It is full of air and fire and water; there is not very much earth.

German critics have seen *A Sad Affair* as a very German book, but it is not without such "un-Germanic" attributes as humor and charm. For all the authentic sadness and earnestness of his pursuit, Friedrich is a borderline comic character. He is, as I think Koeppen was also once described, possibly by himself, "a blithe melancholiac." Koeppen doesn't betray him by mocking him, but he is, shall we say, aware of Friedrich's comic potentialities, his instability, his dither, his unpredictable extremes of modesty and exorbitance: "Sibylle said later that she was convinced that he'd come to shoot her. That was her interpretation of his taut pallor, though there was nothing more behind it than suicide." (This is surely deadpan in every sense.) He is a descendant of the Baudelairean character, the dandy, at once full of conceit and at the same time desperate not to be lower than those he despises. But he is also a softer, less constructed, less *disciplined* character than that; he has no armor and no weapon, no sneer; he tries to be kind and decent and compassionate, even to the likes of Fedor. There is comedy, too, in his intermittent appreciation of the world outside him, where money is raised from friends (if it isn't dropped in the street by bank messengers), or less satisfactorily, by working nights in a lightbulb factory (less restful than it sounds), or selling old clothes one can no longer stand to wear. Or perhaps the whole thing is much simpler than all that: perhaps the idea of so much energy in a character is inherently comic.

A Sad Affair is ingeniously composed, with probably no fewer than three time schemes (or maybe the term *time signatures* would be useful here too): There is the slow progress through the twenty-four hours or so in Zurich; there is a rather more rapid progress through the weeks in Italy; and fastest of all, in a way, are the episodic flashbacks that are dispersed through the narrative (they are fast at least in the way they bring us up to the present, chronologically, through months, if not years). The square brackets encasing further commentary are a likable and ingenious feature; while the rapid intercutting between Friedrich and Sibylle at the time they are both converging on Venice is utterly cinematic (it is even tempting to think of a split screen at that point). Still, the book throughout has a wonderfully "live" feel. It could be an anticipation of a Beat novel, twenty years later. It doesn't feel like a book written with a plan, from hindsight; it feels adventitious, responsive, open to whatever comes up. If a new character happens along—that strange Neapolitan pimp—put him in. If a new setting takes your imagination, write about it: Sibylle's time in the stiflingly bourgeois world of German provincial repertory theater, where "she suffered nightmares of oversize traffic policemen." If you notice something out of the corner of your eye, don't leave it out: Italian women, "their blue-painted eyelids demurely cast down, and their mouths a shocking red," or drums being carried "in the raw red hands of long-armed young men with unpleasant coughs." It's how someone writes who is in love with writing, who discovers he has talent, senses he can do anything, meet any challenge. This, almost as much as the entanglement with Sibylle, is the story of *A Sad Affair*. In some ways, it's not such a sad affair at all.

Michael Hofmann
Albinen, Valais
July 2002

A Sad Affair

IT WAS the first time Friedrich had ever crossed a border into another country. That said, the idea of borders was not new to him. As a child in a war-ravaged village behind a line of fortifications to the east, he had seen a border go up in flames. Later on, as a young man, in the town on the coast, he had often climbed the lofty spire of St. Nicholas to gaze across the sea, where in the flickering air between water and sky you could follow the ships, till πway out they merged into the haze of the horizon and became invisible, so that only your longing could accompany them beyond the line of red buoys that marked the limits of the territorial waters, and out onto the deep swell. Those were borders, the one a nightmarish display of smoke and flames, devastation and dead horses impaled on ripped wire entanglements, and the other beckoning like a dream of distance. This new border, though, was different again, it was marked by passport and customs controls, alien uniforms and language, official stamp and jingle of unfamiliar coins, a switch of locomotive to pull the train that as it snuffled on, surprised you by pulling scenery past the window that seemed like the identical twin sister of the scenery of the homeland you had just left behind. Hills and valleys under a thin layer of snow, green winter wheat, people on the streets, houses, villages, animals, cars and bicyclists all familiar and jolly, until night descended, and in the darkness, the country seemed to acquire a rougher aspect. And then the train pulled into the renowned foreign city.

As he set down his suitcase on the platform, he asked himself whether the city whose name he read on the platform was his final destination or just a way station on his progress south. It was his intention to go on traveling south, and he had in his pocket a ticket that would take him farther; but it was his desire [his secret desire, that he hadn't admitted to anyone] to be welcomed here, and to be permitted to stay.

Sibylle was living in the foreign city. She had written to him, and he had seen her name in the newspaper as well, in a review of a troupe of actors that she belonged to. He had come on her account. She was the only person he knew in the city. It was idle to hope that she might have been on the platform to greet him. He knew that she was not fond of arrangements that compelled her attendance in a certain place at a certain time, yes, that she suffered from them, as a child suffered from having to go to school, and he had therefore been careful not to tell her the time of his arrival, or even the date of it.

He thought of telephoning but reflected that it was getting on for eight o'clock, and that Sibylle would most likely be on her way to the theater. As he wandered through the station hall, suitcase in hand, he thought he was probably the picture of indecision. Hotel agents came up to him, appraised him from his hat to his heels, which were probably somewhat worn, and commended their various establishments to him. But what did those names mean to him? Did he know whether he could afford the Grand Hotel, beside the lake? Or was the Three Kings more realistic? He wanted to see Sibylle. Of course he did. She was staying at St. Peter's Hostel, and that was the name he finally gave the taxi driver.

The streets were full of light and life. I am wealthy, proclaimed the city. It wished for visitors to know. The street that led away from the station was a kind of fanfare. The city had remained neutral during the War, unscathed by shells and crises, spared any reparations, war debts, and inflation, its banks stood there like fortresses sure. Gray massive stone structures, wrought-iron grilles in front of the windows and doors, caryatids representing the god Mercury and the giant Atlas climbed ornamentally up the facades, all compressed into a strongbox, just as Thomas Cook's travelers check bureaux were depicted on the witty posters in the form of a handy suitcase: Your traveler's check is the bank in your pocket. Then came glittering plateglass windows. Jewelers, tailors, luxury leather goods of crocodile, snakeskin, and buffalo, and carefully softened lights caressing silk from Lyons. Friedrich took it all in, rolling about in his barge of a taxi, while the horns of enormous, black-lacquered, powerful droning limousines wailed on all sides, and, just as they were about to turn up a little side street, he once more felt uncertain, felt anxious, wondered whether it would be sensible to take a room at the St. Peter's right next to Sibylle's. Everything was so unpredictable, and the terror that Sibylle had represented to him, and that perhaps was still only dormant, could perhaps take possession of him again, if they were staying in adjacent rooms. Hurriedly, he drew aside the little window to the driver's cab, and said: "I'm sorry, I've changed my mind," and gave him the name of the big hotel on the lake instead.

The change of mind, initially, felt like a liberation. It meant a prolongation of the drive that demanded nothing of him other than that he accept a reposeful confinement while progress was made on his behalf. From the long curve of a bridge, tall arc lamps cast part of their shimmer on the lake to either side, along whose right-hand shore the road was now leading. Through chinks in the doors and windows a smell of damp now came in and mingled with the faint smells of petrol and rubber inside the taxi. Over the shore promenade on the opposite side, fog lamps flowered in milky bubbles of glass. Wraiths of mist rose in wild dances from the black mirroring water. To look out from the shore onto the deep was to catch an intimation of monsters. As one gurgling wave climbed over another, it was as though a human being had been thrown into that maelstrom, was dragged in the undertow, until bubbles rose up, and he finished tethered to the spongy bed of some hibernating amphibious creature. The chauffeur was driving faster now, the car skidded on the slick asphalt, the city seemed to want to go on forever, and suddenly Friedrich was afraid his hotel would be too far away from the action.

Even though his room was pricey, it looked cheap. The hotel management, one could see why, had amused itself by installing a penal cell for second-class guests whose meager circumstances meant that their holdings were entered in no bank, that they didn't belong in this hotel, and had overstretched themselves by coming here. There were grilles in front of the window here too, but in this case they had probably been put there to keep the occupant from the temptation to leap clear not only of an unpaid bill but of all the other demands a life might put on him.

In the hall page boys had stood with scarlet facings on white satiny uniforms. They were the equerries of the lord [who sat enthroned on a lofty dais in formal black], and had been chosen for their straight bearing and their comeliness, gifts that they made much of in their gait and their expression. They were terrestrial angels, bathed and scrubbed, sweet boys who played soccer outside the kitchen windows when they weren't on duty in the lobby or the corridors with the ice-blue eyes of an old extortioner over the last silverware of a terminally ill widow. They took receipt of the guest on his arrival, forming a cordon that conducted him quite irresistibly to the head porter. He in turn waited in the cheerful attitude of an American film star, of whom every child knows that under his respectable jacket he is packing a gun. He asked how long the guest cared to stay, for a longer sojourn it might be necessary to apply to the Police Prefecture for permission .

This is a mistake, Friedrich realized, and it's not bringing me any nearer to her. Behind the window bars was the magnificent and silent lake, an eerie field under drizzly fog and uncertain illumination. There were no mountains to be seen but they must be there, obscured by the dark, pure white crowns, above the clouds, clearly visible from under the stars.

I'm not going to turn up there, I'll send a note, he thought. Friedrich was afraid he might suffer bedazzlement in the theater, lightnings that would unambiguously expose the falsity of his position here, find himself thrown out and blinded and back in the maelstrom of terrible need, out of which, injured, certainly, he had thought he had managed to drag himself. I'll send her a note, she can write back, and we'll meet somewhere that's not a jungle of stage props. He suggested she might like to have lunch with him in a bright, friendly café of her choosing. He rang, the way a gentleman rings in a big hotel, and gave one of the precocious pages an instruction to take a letter to the Diana Variety and wait for a reply. Then he turned on a thick stream of water from the gold-colored faucet that flowed into the marble shower-bath and stuck his head under it, snorting under the bubbles and froth.

Once he had rubbed himself dry, he tried to wait patiently. He wanted to remain calm, to pace back and forth, hum a tune, but his heart wasn't playing. It was skipping in his breast, and sometimes it leapt up into his mouth—hurrah, hurrah—it was hard to bear. He took out the telephone directory of the foreign city and read the names of strange people. Then he envied anyone who might live here, be it as a dentist or a plumber, because it looked as though the troupe and Sibylle would be remaining in the city for a good while yet. He still loved her, then, that was certain, and it didn't come as a surprise to him. He had never ceased to love her, but his passion with all its peaks and troughs had grown calmer once Sibylle had left and stayed away. It is my destiny to love her, and I must accept it. That had become his conviction, the scrap of comfort that he clung to, ever since he had attempted to pull a star down from the sky to be accepted by her. She, however, had not accepted him, not caught him, but let him lie there with a broken back, and then not before shouting to a few people who happened to be listening as she turned away, "There lies the man who wanted to pluck me a star from the sky!" And he had writhed on the ground like a worm.

It was too awful to contemplate, if she reacted negatively to his letter this time. It had been wrong of him to write, but simply turning up wouldn't have been right either. It was a hopeless situation. But was it certain that she would react negatively? He would act a part now, that of the man who's had enough, who stops by on his way to more important errands and more ravishing adventures to see, just out of curiosity really, how an old girlfriend is keeping. Then the hotel might be a good place to start from after all—if only the attitude, the point of view, had been genuine. He wavered again. Was she not tender and sweet? Just a girl really? And everything else awful misunderstandings that, once they had been cleared up, would no longer darken his sky?

At ten o'clock the scarlet-and-white-satin page boy knocked on the door, and pushed no letter into the hand that Friedrich extended. He said: "The lady will be waiting for you at the stage door at half past eleven tomorrow morning." That was both a bombshell and a relief, just as he was feeling a little less shaky, and it gave him an excuse to leave his room and go out into the unfamiliar city.

The Diana Variety, they said, was in the Old Town. He walked along the shore, in the direction of the lights, and all the chill off the lake, which so far he had felt only through the windows, now blew in his face. By the time he reached the frosted railing of the long, wide bridge, he was already chilled to the marrow. He felt as though the cold had thrown dank nooses of cold water at him. He was trembling, but that might also be attributable to his excitement. He stopped to ask a passerby for directions and couldn't get a word out. The man looked at him and took a step away, fearfully and suspiciously. At last Friedrich was able to blurt out "Diana" like a cry. The man stepped nearer and laughed. He said: "Straight on, and then it's up the lane on your right." Friedrich thought: He'd like to pat me on the back. The man's expression showed solidarity. "You don't need to be ashamed of yourself, we're pretty tolerant people here," and with those words he went off.

The lane on the right was crooked and old. The gabled houses recalled old Frankfurt and the docklands of Hamburg, districts for which Friedrich felt a romantic affection, and yet he was surprised to find the Variety in what was probably a poor area. All around there were bars. Tinted lights twinkled behind curtained windows. Each time a door opened, there was a warm whiff of people, beer, wine, cigar smoke, and the sweat of bustling waitresses. The pubs were so packed, they seemed about to burst, and Friedrich had the sense that when a door opened, all those within grabbed hold of each other so as not to fall out. There were little clusters of people that wanted to remain as they were. Whereas there was hardly anyone out on the pavement. It was hard to say how people went into the pubs, or left them. Did they use back entrances that led into the courtyards of other buildings, had they come up through trapdoors, or could it be that this clientele had arrived early and planned on spending the night? A policeman stood out. In his cloak he resembled a snail in its carapace of shell. He was protected, nothing could befall him, he stared indifferently into the gutter at his feet, and Friedrich once more asked: "Diana?"

The policeman put out his arm, "Over there!" and a white baton jerked out in the appropriate direction. "Over there!" were some luminous letters, clambering up a wall. The eye first had to get used to the rhythm, and then it was able to read: DIANA VARIETY THEATER.

Now what did that mean: a basement and a main entrance? In the vitrine next to the main entrance were pictures of an unambiguous nature. Groups of girls, naked save for a sparkling little *rien* round their loins, the ghost of a pair of knickers, a puff of material that was just enough for the eyes to seize upon, so that a minimum of imagination, the little bit that the johns here might manage to muster, would suffice to suggest to the brain what further strippings, colorings, games, and surprises might be possible. And also, there was the strong man with the dumbbells extended high above his head, bulges of muscle under his bursting singlet, and there was the chanteuse with heavy gray face and décolletage, and sparkling glass cherries in her water-waved hair.

But Sibylle! Where was she? He pressed his face against the glass, he could taste makeup and the salt of tears, and he felt his way through the faces, one after another, and he saw round cows' eyes, empty, willing faces, teasingly curled fingers, expressions miming desire, worn mouths; it was disgusting. He felt himself blush. Blush, here, where no one knew him. A man walked past, and he wondered: What must he take me for? But only for a second. And then once more: Sibylle! But where was she? This couldn't be the troupe she was acting in. That was impossible. The

newspaper in which he had read the review would never have written up the sort of scenes that stared up at him from behind the
glass. Then he saw the basement entrance, and there, way down, so
that you had to bend down to see it, was another vitrine.

A child's face, a little melancholy, that was her, and the other one,
jaunty in her blue-and-white-striped school pinafore, that was her
as well. "Sibylle," and there it was again, the muted tone in his
voice as it whispered in her ear, and he felt the hair stand up on his
neck, and he loved her, and he hoped her hands would still be a little grubby, and her fine, deft fingers, when he leaned down to kiss
them, would still smell of colored sweets and sweetish herb vinegar.

"Ah' tu es belle!" someone had written across the juncture of her
cheek and neck. *"Ah' tu es belle!"*; the fellow must have pushed his
pen between the bars to do it, the glass was smashed there, and he
must have taken quite some trouble to write it: *"Ah' tu es belle!"* He
should be pleased. She would say: "It makes you miserable if people like me." But he was pleased. He even laughed to himself. But
he was afraid, a little, for the man who had written it. She smiled.
An Italian might have written *"O belle dolce."* Her colleagues
alongside her looked pretty grim. A woman with a shapely Roman
head. Young men and women in sweaters, because that was the
style. The whole thing had a somewhat Russian effect. It could be
a basement cabaret in Moscow, to say it right out, but, to say it even
more clearly, it wasn't.

Then they all came out. People, so many people. It was baffling
that so many people could have been accommodated in that cellar.
But they looked neither rumpled nor exhausted. They wore good
coats, and the women had fashionable hats. Some even disap-

peared into the cars that had suddenly driven up, purring, from all different directions. If you'd asked him, Friedrich would have replied that it was people from the educated middle classes who had come up from the depths.

He himself descended. Or perhaps rather, he thought he would. He needed some willpower to walk down the steps and enter the premises. A buffet seemed to have been set up in the anteroom. Cloakroom attendants and waiters were reckoning up with a fat man behind the bar. A girl was shouting angrily. It was something about the number of paintings by some artists that had been sold. The girl was getting unpleasantly heated. She was arguing over a small sum of money, as if her life depended on it. She belonged to the troupe, she was in fact the cashier who traveled with them wherever they went.

Friedrich would have had to cross the anteroom to reach the theater proper, but it felt like a barricade he didn't dare cross. He also had an apprehension that the cashier's sharp voice would snap at him, even after the performance was over, and, with passionate professionalism, demand money from him for a ticket. Not that he would have minded about the money, but he was ashamed of having imagined a scene where he would pay up rather than make a fuss, and without needing to, without it even being sensible. Instead, he stopped at the buffet and ordered a drink, so as to justify his presence there in some way.

And that was still the state of play when a young fellow came out of the theater, one of the ones he had seen outside in sweaters, and he walked up to Friedrich and shook his hand. "Come with me," he said, and there was something in his voice that sounded pleased and welcoming. Friedrich followed him into the theater, and felt oppressed by some premonition, even before he had any firm idea of what was going on. "Here he is," called the young man in the sweater, once they'd crossed the room, which was like a battlefield strewn with chairs, "here he is, and here," he said, pointing up at the stage, "is Sibylle." Who straightway came bounding through the gap in the curtains, jumped down, laughed, gave Friedrich her hand, casual, lovable, familiar: "So there you are, you old so-and-so!" And then: "Have you two met, I thought you might know Fedor," and then Friedrich did remember, and he remembered cafés and night clubs and a young Russian who had sung songs about hunger and revolution in a low bass voice, Fedor, the man in the sweater—and he turned to look at him.

And then others came down from the stage as well: the Roman girl; the rough form of a peasant woman from olden days; a lanky albino chap with watery eyes; Anja, a little girl bundled up in a sheepskin, the clown in the troupe, now coughing and rapidly drawing on a cigarette in her soft mouth. They all clustered around Friedrich, welcomed him, and asked him for news of home, as they called the country he had just left, although to them, Russian émigrés from the wave of 1917, it could hardly have been home. Fedor took charge, he spoke for Friedrich, gave answers on his behalf to questions [to which Friedrich had not collected himself] and finally said *"Du"* to him, taking his arm with a generous, fraternal gesture: "What do you want to drink, let's have a bite to eat, come and join us at the buffet."

A long table had been set up, at which members of the troupe but also other persons were sitting. People who weren't directly

involved with the cabaret but were somehow friends or hangers-on,
who got a meal ticket from one or other member. Friedrich saw
faces that looked tense, hungry, and unsure. "They are refugees,"
he said to himself, and then he thought: But the czar's no longer
alive, so why are they sitting here in the basement chewing their
bread like anarchists on the eve of the great day when they will take
the bomb they've hidden in their coat, and throw it at the feet of
the horses drawing the Imperial carriage? There was a measure of
repugnance and disapproval in Friedrich. He felt bourgeois, which
he hadn't really before, a man who acted by the lights of reason and
sense. "Perhaps I'm in a bad mood," he said to himself. "Something
is predisposing me against these people." He was not a loudmouth.
He wasn't happy to have to talk to strangers, with a lot of people he
didn't know, of whom he knew only what he thought he saw, and
whose society he had not sought. Principally, however, had he come
here to sit so far away from Sibylle, who was only one of the voices
in the general conversation? He was sitting next to her, he had at
least managed that, but could he do more than look at her from the
side? Questions, questions. She smells of something. Maybe it's old
greasepaint grown rancid. She looks excited. How did she fall in
with these people in the first place? She's no Russian, she's from
the west, I'm more of an Easterner than she is.

"Can we go?" he said.

And she: "Where to, everything here closes at midnight."

He hung his head. Do I still desire her? I can't even say whether
I find her attractive. Her face doesn't have the power it once had,
to fling me to the ground. I have an actress next to me, a member
of a troupe of savages, who seem intent on conferring the gamy

taste of darkness to everything they do. Now Anja over there, the soft round face above the shaggy white sheepskin, and the tired expression of a child still awake at the end of the party, I could feel some tenderness for. Whereas Sibylle, why? All right then, then it'll be over, I'll go home to my hotel, and tomorrow I'll travel on, have a wonderful time, see the south and the sun and the sea.

"Where are you staying?"

The question was from Fedor, and he was thrown into a panic. He said: "The Grand Hotel," and he said it quietly, and he saw, before anyone was able to say anything, that it was something to be ashamed of. He explained: "It was the only hotel I knew by name, and I wanted to be right on the lake."

Sibylle asked: "How long are you staying for?"

He said: "Only till tomorrow."

"But we've got so much to talk about, and I wanted to go out with you somewhere!"

Her face was turned toward him now, and he saw it plainly, and he scraped away layers of what might be the bad air in this smoky room till she was the way he remembered her. Her mouth was without lipstick, and he thought: She used to take more care of herself. But then he thought that that was probably inevitable, because whom did she have to look after her? He felt like taking her hands between his and warming them, as if they had been those of a child that has fallen into the water and is lying on the stones of the quayside, trembling and pale, while the heroic policeman has left home, left wife and child and mother [and left the group photographs on his walls], and gone out in a boat after her, pulled her out with a boat hook, getting himself thoroughly wet in the process, and gives the alarm.

There was dismay. The group piped up. "But then you'll miss the performance?"

Friedrich admitted he would, and felt thoroughly rude. To these people, the performance meant everything. And Friedrich wanted to see Sibylle after all, had to see Sibylle. "All right. No, I can stay another day."

A doorman came and said he wanted to close. The fat bartender counted the takings. "We'll buy a bottle of schnapps," said Fedor, "and you can come with us; this is a miserable town, everything closes down at midnight."

And there it was again, his heart was once more in someone else's hand, sometimes they squeezed it shut, sometimes they allowed it to breathe, it wasn't to die on them, a little bird in a cage that had to sing. His chest collapsed, he was close to shaking. "With you?" Of course, when Fedor had fetched him from the buffet and led him into the theater to Sibylle, even then he had known it. And now there were the naked facts. You know there's a pillar in the dark corridor, and still you cry out in shock and pain when you walk into it. *Fedor?* He said: "No, no, I can't bear it, it's too much."

The three of them piled into a cab. Friedrich sat next to Sibylle, Fedor squatted on the foldaway seat opposite them. Once again, it was Friedrich's wish that the drive might go on forever. They zig-zagged through shadows. Into a suburb, a long way from the lake. "Here we are, we'd better give the porter a tip"; the cab stopped; a brass sign winked: ST. PETER'S HOSTEL. "Are you staying here, Sibylle?"

"Of course, you know I am."

"What about Fedor?"

"He is too."

"I'm tired," Friedrich said. "You know, the long journey and everything, I don't want any more to drink, I'll just go home, good night."

Fedor seemed not to understand. He was disappointed. "Hang on, just a minute, I thought we were going to have some fun, celebrate your arrival, Sibylle's so pleased to see you!"

Well, that was nice of Fedor, and Friedrich felt he was much, much older than Fedor, who was certainly no younger than himself, and he said: "Well tomorrow, maybe tomorrow." Then he shook hands with Sibylle and kissed her on the cheek.

"Will you come and get me, ten o'clock, I'm in room fourteen."

"Sure, I'll pick you up, ten o'clock, St. Peter's, room fourteen." He climbed back into the taxi, and drove off. "The Grand Hotel," he managed to say, feeling it might just well have been the lake.

When he awoke, it was seven o'clock and still dark. The passage outside was being swept. A broom scratched at the doormats, shoes were returned from being polished. There was a rumbling of pipes in the walls, the heating came on and still it felt cold. What was he supposed to do? He was pale, and his eyes were wide open, staring up at the ceiling of his cave, and on into infinity.

When I was still living in the Akademiestrasse, I was able to shout and roar like a trapped animal, Friedrich could remember. And that, after just six months, had been what he was reduced to.

WINTER HAD come fierce and early. I had been looking around for a job, probably out of instinct, the way I've often done things to stay alive, things I really didn't want to do, and that I must have done out of instinct, or pure will, or because it was my destiny to go on living, and so I was the tester in a big lightbulb factory in the north of the city. Not a scientifically qualified rank, like the gentlemen who hand in their reports at the patent office, just a low-grade observer, someone who [put in a room full of circuits where thousands upon thousands of electric lightbulbs were coupled to copper rails, and were left to burn night and day, giving out a dry, stinging, disagreeable heat] had to watch and write down the time when a bulb burned out. The university's labor exchange had fixed me up with that when I'd gone looking for some night work. They said: "You're a literature student, but for this you just need eyes in your head."

I had pictured the job as being pleasanter than it turned out to be. I thought I would have leisure to think about one or two things that had been occupying me for some time. I had assumed the night in the lamp room of the sleeping factory would be like a watch on a clipper ship, gliding along under the trade winds, bringing peace and contemplation to even the most neurotic characters. In the end I had to pay attention like a hawk. Even though I wore dark glasses, I found the light dazzling. I ran around like a madman, investigating shadows that turned out to be purely imaginary, in constant danger of being caught napping by some works inspector, or in an excess of zeal getting too close to one of the heavily laden copper circuits and receiving a possibly fatal shock.

Also, it turned out to be a disadvantage, more psychologically than actually, that I understood so little of how the place functioned technically, because before long I lived in terror of some unforeseen accident, something that an expert would be able to remedy safely and perfectly easily, but to someone with my ignorance less easy and, in fact, potentially catastrophic. A short circuit, a failure in the transformer unit, a spark in the oil switch, bits of equipment that were nothing but names to me but still names that stood in some relation to various catastrophes, these made me tremble, and I carefully memorized the route to the alarm, so that in the event of my being plunged into darkness—deeper and more impenetrable darkness than you could find anywhere else in the world—even then, I would be sure to find it. Following these exertions, I came home in the morning exhausted, in an empty streetcar with three empty carriages attached to it to bring workers to the factory district when the shift came on, rumbling through the gloaming, and then to bed with the morning paper, which slipped from my grasp, sleeping, sometimes dreaming of the time clock with its cogs, until from the yard that my room opened on, the beating of carpets and the calls of the rag and bottle men would wake me.

For this, as it transpired, enervating work I was paid a hundred marks per month. That represented my entire income. Except for what I needed to pay for my room, I had all day to spend it in.

I got up at around noon and went into art school, not to study but to eat. There was a cafeteria there that was a little bit the way I imagine a bohemian restaurant in nineteenth-century novels. You could watch them come down from their ateliers in their paint-spattered overalls, their faces still radiant with creativity, casually picking a bowl off the rack and taking huge mouthfuls, and with them their models, noisy and full of themselves, and showing in their faces, too, some association with paint.

It was in this cafeteria, which was always lively and always full, that I first met Beck. That is, I'd met him before, but this was where we got to know each other properly. In the summer I'd been swimming in the river near where Beck lived, and, not knowing the currents, I would have drowned if Beck hadn't pulled me onto his boat as he happened to be passing. He saved my life, I suppose you could say, although he hadn't done much beyond grabbing hold of me when he saw I was in trouble. And then, as luck would have it, Beck knew the man I was staying with, who specialized in fish paintings. They were all over the walls, these fishes, fishes out of water and fishes swimming; the painter would stand in front of them and stretch, and his hair would shoot up into the air, and he would say: "My paaaintings," and as he said the long *a* sound, he would stick out his tongue. Beck supported this painter by bringing him food from his mother's kitchen. From that point on, I referred to Beck as the art dealer, because I thought, as later proved to be the case, that he had a gift for these art-related business transactions. But the real reason for his fondness for the fish painter, and this speaks for him [and will always, whatever happens, speak for him], was that he wanted to see another picture that was hidden behind the fish paintings, and which had so far escaped my notice. This was no paaainting [tongue stuck out during the long *a* sound] but a pastel of a delicacy and feeling that one would not have thought the artist had had in him, a pastel of a girl, little more than a child, leaning against a chimney breast with a lyre in her hand, dressed like a fairy-tale prince. And that was Sibylle! Her parents lived in a country house a little way upriver, and the painter had been to visit them. He said the girl had been ill at the time and sitting up in bed and, following a sudden whim, and to cheer her up, he had done the drawing of her as described. I would have liked to have taken it with me, but Beck had a prior claim on it. The model didn't interest me much, and when I left, I learned, not that I was interested, that Sibylle was presently in the capital and would probably make her way in films, and not until Beck one day spoke to me out of the blue in the art school cafeteria, did I remember the Sibylle in the picture.

Beck was agitated. He started talking about Sibylle right away, I didn't have to ask. I was sure he was in love with her. He said: "Please don't laugh, she looks just like an angel." He had gone to see her, bringing greetings from the painter, and she had received him in an apartment that according to his description seemed to be chockablock with cushions and stuffed toys and other movie-starlet flimflam. I didn't like the sound of that, and I supposed she must be a stupid and shallow person. "No, no," Beck replied, "she's just a child!" She had received Beck in a diaphanous robe, and asked him whether she'd done her lipstick right. I had nothing more to say but felt my suspicion of her brainlessness confirmed, when I heard Beck trying to talk to her on the telephone. He picked up the receiver, dialed the number, and said: "Hello, Sibyllchen"; so that meant she was on the other end, and had answered it herself, and what ensued was a dance on coals. Beck was fumbling for words, tried to start up a conversation [just to hear the sound of her voice], but every new topic foundered on her monosyllabic replies.

"It's impossible to talk to her," I observed. "I mean, you can tell; she's nothing but a doll out of a fashion review, an empty-headed creature, and her idea of conversation is some cocktail bar chitchat about the latest cut of the shoulder, or at the most, some matinée idol, and she only talks to well-dressed younger sons of aristos, pimps, or film extras [none of which you are, Beck]." Beck denied this, and we drank wine, wine in the afternoon, though it didn't feel particularly wicked, partly because Beck was so miserable and partly because the wine was some he had brought with him from his own vineyard at home. Then it was time for me to go on to my fairy grotto, and Beck took hold of the bottle he had drunk, broke off its neck, and scrawled "I love you" on the label [Hochberger Kröten-milch], and packed the bottle in a basket and addressed it to Sibylle. He saw me to the streetcar stop on his own way to the post office.

That night I was even more jumpy than usual at work. I had the feeling that the electricity all around was somehow getting to me, and I felt envious of Beck for his wealthy background. I wasn't as bad as I got to be later, when I saw nonexistent sparks and practically yearned for thunderous explosions, but it was certainly a feeling that I'd been warned, that I'd had some notice of the impending calamity.

I'd no sooner gone to bed the following morning than there was a knock on the door, and Beck came into my room. He said: "My dear friend," and for a while that was all, and he walked back and forth. No apology, not a word of explanation, just that pacing to and fro, from the stove to the window, from the window to the stove. I lay there thinking I'm coming down with something. I didn't have the strength to move or to put up any fight, he could have done anything he wanted with me, I just lay still. He had something he wanted to confess, and given time he would speak, but for now he was just pacing back and forth in front of my bed, all I could see were lightbulbs and copper wire and sparks. "I've seen her," he finally said, and came to a stop. "I've seen her, I was in the Volkstheater, up in the circle, and she was sitting down in the stalls. She was with a man whom everybody greeted, he must have been a drama critic, maybe you would have known who he was, you're interested in those kind of people." That sounded hostile to me. He just tossed out that "you're interested in those kind of people" as if writing theater reviews were a contemptible activity, and as if he thought it was just about my level—when only the day before he'd had to loan me a couple of marks. Then he suddenly jerked upward with a cry of rage, picked a book off my bedside table, and flipped it up in the air. "Do you think," he yelled, "do you think she's sleeping with him?"

Of course I thought she was, and I thought it must be a nice thing to sleep with someone. I was perfectly candid with him, but I wasn't thinking about sex. I had never felt solitude so keenly as it revealed itself to me now. There I was, lying between my already dusty sheets, and in front of me there was a man getting all steamed up about something. What was my connection with him? I lay there, as though on insulating layers. Who would care if I died? Oh, if only there were another human being lying at my side, so that I could feel another's breath, another's heart, the feeling of another's skin, the stirrings of some dream that wasn't mine, because even my dreams were dreadful.

"Of course she's sleeping with him," I said to Beck. "He'll want that and require it of her, because the life of the mind doesn't make anyone happy, not even a critic; and didn't you yourself say Sibylle was beautiful and sexy?"

Yes, I was crude. I admit I was, and I can completely understand Beck stalking out of the room with a glare that pierced me to the marrow, that's how hurt he was, and slamming the door in a fury. "I'm ill!" I shouted after him, but probably he didn't hear me. Why did he have to come to me with his grief? I had no experience of these matters. Grief, yes, but not love. On that morning, I was of the view that not having a piece of bread in the house was a far, far worse thing altogether.

I can't remember if I managed to get off to sleep after that. All I know is that at about noon I got up, feeling shaky and tired, and did one or two exercises in the cold room [I couldn't afford heating], without really believing they accomplished anything. Finally, I began to shave; and even that with a hollow feeling of duty and habit, unenthusiastic, and not expecting the least improvement to come from the activity. Damnit, it was the beginning of a fatuous day which was certain to end as fatuously. I decided I would devote myself to my studies again, and hang on to my nighttime job; what else was I going to live off? But I had to find a way of getting through it that didn't take so much out of me.

I still had my face full of shaving foam when there was a knock. "*Avanti*," I called out, because poor people have nothing to fear from a surprise. "*Avanti*, come on in," and I sounded a lot more chipper than I felt. I was surprised to see Beck walk in. I hadn't expected him back following this morning's scene, and I had already decided I would apologize the next time I saw him in the cafeteria. As he stopped in the doorway, I supposed that he too felt the awkwardness of the situation, and I called out once more: "Please come in, there's a draft, and I'm sorry I'm not dressed yet,

I haven't felt well all day." The apology for my being undressed and the reference to feeling unwell was also intended to cover and apologize for my rudeness earlier that morning. But Beck was still hanging back in the doorway, I wanted to reach out my hand to him and pull him into the room, but then behind him in the dark corridor I heard giggling, and laughter, and finally loud laughter, and then he got a shove from behind, that was unmistakable, because he stumbled in and fell, fell right on top of the chair that had all my clothes on it, which he promptly upset, my God they were dusty, and who would brush them for me, and then I heard another voice: "Come on, he's an idiot, you can see that, hello, I wanted to visit you," and a hand was extended in my direction, and behind it there emerged from the darkness an arm, a dress, a body, a neck and head and eyes and a mouth [especially a mouth], and there was Sibylle standing in my room, a little shorter than me, and smiling and lovely.

It was the first time in my life that I found myself thinking and acting utterly conventionally. I felt sandbagged or hexed, I mean, I could have been the headmaster of the Christian Ladies' Academy of the Sacred Heart. I saw Sibylle in front of me, and my true nature showed perhaps a little in my look, I looked at her, looked past the disguise of the ladies' hat, and past the ruff at her throat, I disregarded them, and I saw her figure and her face, I saw her hands, and if I'd been able to think at that moment, then I would have thought: Yes, but God sees into the heart. I knew everything, none of what happened later remotely surprised me. I knew: I love her, I love her! But my room! That ugly furnished room at the back of the house, the wallpaper tent, sun-bleached and full of sputum and bedbugs. The bareness and the poverty. I saw them as well. And my stubble under the drying soap. And the heap of possible/impossible clothes on the floor, and the decrepit chair and the narrow bed. It all seemed terribly important suddenly, which normally it didn't at all. I looked around at everything, and finally, out of the paralysis that had befallen me, I stammered: "Here, please, won't you sit down!" The formal "*Sie*" I stressed, as if I were giving orders to a whole regiment. It surprises me today, after I've spent many hours thinking about the state of paralysis I got into then, that I didn't actually go on to say "Miss," but that must have been just a little too remote from me then as an idea, otherwise I'm certain I would have done it.

The way I behaved, in keeping with my sudden paralysis, was clear and logical. I was stiff and remote. I picked a tie off the floor, though not in order to tie it round my neck. Instead, I made it into a sling, and then dangled my arm in it. Only after this bizarre carrying-on did I turn to her again—she hadn't sat down on the chair I'd offered, but had lain down on my bed as if she wanted to sleep [which maybe, who knows, she did]—and said: "Forgive me for not shaking hands with you, the fact is I've just broken my arm." I said it with a perfectly straight face, nor is it my impression that anyone laughed.

But my humiliation still had a lot further to go. I saw myself as the most wretched of men, living in a crumbling hut, with ocher streams of sewage swilling round it. I had never had a girl in my room, and now here was a young lady stretched out on my bed, practically purring like a young cat wanting milk, and her skirts had ridden up, she was wearing kneesocks and I was tormented by the thought [as if I didn't have enough on my mind]: Where was it again that I read the line, "Dorian maiden, with thighs exposed!"? And that was followed by a further stream of associations: Greek temples, stadia, athletes' limbs, bowls of wine and roses wreathed in hair. Also I could see the scene again, on a lake up in the east, in slant, reddish evening light and against the backdrop of black pine forests, the young fellows from the sawmill riding the horses into the water, naked and shining on the gleaming wet hide of the snorting animals.

"Walter's not home tonight, he's been asked to a premiere, so why don't we go out together for supper, and maybe go on to Aunt Molly's afterward." She seemed to be speaking to herself, and I can't help but think of a cat, purring from deep within, its claws retracted, warm and expectant. So she was going to go on to Aunt Molly's. That was news to me. I had never been there myself, but I had heard of it. It had a bad reputation, and people whose purpose it served to appear disreputable liked to meet there. I said: "I'm afraid I can't go, I'm busy at night." [God knows, I didn't want to go either, in my stained suit and with no money in my pocket, it was bad enough her seeing me in the one I had on.]

Then she said: "You're ill." And pointing to the sling with my arm in it, "And you're a cripple!"

It was true. At the moment of my first encounter with Sibylle, I got in the habit of feeling crippled with indecision. It happened to me then. I hobbled across the room, exaggeratedly, like a ham, dragging one foot after, stooped and skewed. The worst of it was that Beck, who up until now had been leaning pale and angry against the cold stove, now got the bug and started limping as well.

We wandered through the room, a couple of beggars out for a stroll, and, without any rehearsal or arrangement, fell into a grim sport, taking turns at being big and small, now face-to-face, now at opposite ends of the room. Any sane person would have thought we had lost it, but there wasn't a sane person in the room. Sibylle observed us unsmilingly, but pleasantly. She was like a child who has just been given a new toy and is still perplexed, wondering how to play with it. Her face seemed to be inclined over us, even if it was actually lower than we were, walking, and I think the way we were looking up at her was like puppets at the puppet-mistress who was holding our strings.

"Now what about tonight?" she asked. And to me in particular: "You're ill, you don't need to be a doctor to see that." Beck nodded. I insisted I wasn't, and began to wish they would both leave, so I could quickly go and lie down on the bed that presently had Sibylle on it. Beck said something to that effect, and asked Sibylle to come away. "I won't hear of it, I'm tired, I want to rest," and suddenly she was almost furious, and crossly turned her face to the wall. Beck went purple, and I wanted to say something nice to him, but I couldn't think of anything. Then Sibylle suddenly yelled: "Leave me alone, you moron, and stop staring at me!"

Naturally, Beck pulled the door open and stomped off. Or at least that day, it still seemed the natural thing to do. What else was a man to do? But for me it was probably the last day of these natural thoughts. I felt sorry for Beck, much more than I had done before. And I even thought: This is awful. And stood, still half-shaved, by my bed, which had Sibylle lying in it, a girl who had come to me in much the same way as, when you're still very young, you imagine children coming into the world: all of a sudden they're lying on your bed, or somebody's, and they're there.

I didn't yet know, and how could I have known, I wasn't a psychologist and I hadn't had the experience either, I was always, not exactly lonely, but at least solitary, so I didn't know yet that it was young Sibylle's way [when I met her she had just turned seventeen], her destiny if you like, to fall in love with people that others had told her about, often quite zany particulars. And that was what Beck had done about me. And on top of that she was so perverse—she told me that later, when I was quite done in, and needed picking up; oh, she just made life worse, really—that the midden I was living in, my bad suit trousers, and my features that looked ill nourished, all struck her as the essence of grime, to which she, in a different and lascivious orbit at this time of her life [it was a life of luxury, Cockaigne, she was going out with the famous drama critic] felt attracted. Yes, her mouth offered itself to me, and that item of consolation unhinged me! I have never kissed it, but in that hour of ostensibly my lowest humiliation, I could have become someone else, another man in pomp and glory! Yes, if I had lain down at her side then—I could have become a sailor or a revolutionary, a folk hero, a flag-bearer for definite, and the cynosure of all eyes, because, since I didn't become any of these things, I feel that if I had gone to her, I would have had to have become radiant for all eternity. I didn't, and I'm gray, an uninteresting traveler carrying a suitcase whose colorful labels are merely the evidence of meaningless journeys.

I needed to do something for Beck. I flung myself on the idea like a dog on a bone. I loved her, but first of all I needed to do some gnawing on Beck's behalf. And the silly ladies' hat lying next to her: I couldn't stand ladies. I said: "You should wear children's hats!"

"Sure!" She agreed right away, dismissed the hat as the drama critic's idea.

"Why?"

And then she told me: "Well, you know," and she said she would just count up the number of people she had been unfaithful to him with, and she counted the whole of the known world [I didn't know any of them], and then she concluded: "So it's not too much to ask really, he loves me so much, Walter does, that I might as well do him a favor with the hat, since he cares about it so much."

She wasn't a monster either. I was only given proof of that much later. "Well," I said, back then, "you know [and I kept with the '*Sie*', I clung to it like a shipwrecked man clinging to a mast], you know Beck is crazy with desire for you, so why don't you add another one to the number of horns you're making your master wear, and it would be a good deed too?"

"I don't want to do any good deeds!"

Aha, that was the explanation. Beck had offered himself in the wrong way. You couldn't play the abject Werther[1] card with her. I could see that. A reluctance came over her words that made the case appear hopeless.

"I can't," she went on to say. "What do you think? If I don't want to, I can't; surely you can understand that."

And it's true, I've never met a woman who was less able to give herself against her own will than Sibylle. But that understanding took

---

[1] A reference to Goethe's novel *The Sorrows of Young Werther* (1774).

a long time to arrive as well. I was still at the stage of getting everything confused. I was so stupid, I even asked: "Then why do you go
out with Beck; why do you torment him and get his hopes up?"

"Oh, you know, it's like this," [and she purred again], "everyone
wants something from me ever since I've been here, and Beck who
comes from my home, by the river where I come from too, I
thought with him he didn't want anything. Just someone to have
fun with. You know, I need that. Of course he'd like to sleep with
me as well, everybody does, but that's silly, isn't it? You'd like to,
too, wouldn't you?"

The leap once more from Beck to me, Alcibiades' question to
Socrates. I didn't say, but I was all atwitter in my lark's nest. "Well
now, Miss, I need to go now, I've got to go to work, all night, yes,
no, I'm not ill, I can't afford to be ill, I'm the night watchman!" I
acted terribly mysterious over my silly lightbulb job. She made a
moue, I don't like the word, I think it's horrid, but she pouted, it felt
like that to me, I have to use a teenage word to get that across,
damnit, if only I'd had a sister, I thought at the time, I've never
been around girls in my life.

I left, it really was high time if I was to get to work, and she
stayed behind in my room, in my bed. "There's the key for the front
door," I said, "but please don't lose it, I'll come and collect it, by the
time I get back tomorrow morning, the front door'll be open
already, so good-bye."

HAVING REACHED which point in his thinking about his relationship with Sibylle [it was the abiding problem, it was quite

impossible to think enough about it, and to obtain clarity, and grasp the law that governed his life], having thought his way back to the instant when he left her asleep for the first time [in his room, in his bed], to go to the factory, to earn his wages, which before long he gave up doing, at a time when it made even less sense to miss anything, even the most foolish duty, over his wooing of Sibylle—having reached which point in his painful reflections, an inspection of his own person in the gray sequence of a reverie, Friedrich lying in his bed in the hotel in the foreign city, awaiting the morning, shouted out loud, and flung himself on the pillows next to him with the air of a man fallen off his steed into the mud, trying to bury himself in it away from the hooves. The gates of life were slammed shut. Forever. Behind him. He himself had thrown them shut. With every step he had taken, with every step to the garish lamp room in the bulb factory. He believed firmly, he had that in him, no hands could clutch a monstrance as tightly [and sometimes he prayed, contemned, in the back of churches], that it was his destiny and his vocation, and that Sibylle was intended for none but himself, and that a misunderstanding [oh, how he clung to the word: *misunderstanding*!], a serious error of feeling—he cried out, but Sibylle couldn't hear, she was always far away, always on the opposite shore, even when she was near—was to blame for everything. Sometimes he thought: Maybe it's like building a tunnel, Sibylle started digging over there, and I started here, according to the architect's plans we should have met, but then all we did was get close to one another; she heard the jab of my pick, and I took in the scrape of her shovel, the earth was already beginning to crumble, the layer separating us was finger-thin—and then I was blinded with folly, and I changed the direction in which I was digging, I drove my tunnel into the deep, toward the glowing kernel, toward Hell, the way it's depicted in old paintings.

It all happened, this has to be emphasized, so dispassionately, so sternly and juridically. It happened like this: he set off for his lamp room, saw the evening lights come on in the street, they seemed to be readying the area for a party, women dressed in the ceremonial robes of the Stuart queens peered out of shiny automobiles on to the sidewalk, the commissionaires swung their sticks in front of the portals of theaters and restaurants with their veiled windows. In this part of town, which Friedrich only ever passed through, they were mounting a production of mankind in all its wealth and glory. Even the newspaper crier was participating, relaying with faintly bloodcurdling shouts the distant tremor of the ground under our feet from some epicenter away in the east that only reaches our seismographs in the form of a gentle, feeble wave, which we need to enjoy life to the full. He blazoned out the tragedy, "Jewel Theft!" he roared—oh, what a tragedy. So the jewels had been plucked off a white throat, some black fingers had reached out and taken them, and now the lady was weeping, and the insurance company was cursing; aside from them, who cared, who could eat off the stones, who could be made happy by them? But the newspaper was of the opinion that a jewel theft is a sensation. Friedrich passed on his way. The street ahead, and the street behind. In the street behind, they weren't so interested in the humbug of the evening edition. Here, people moved forward in masses, and, for the time being, against one another. One ought to join in, participate, feel concerned! Thus Friedrich, that evening. At least while he was on his way to work. Then the factory. The entry had been built in such a way that one had little option but to slip into it. No one could walk on by when the opening was agape. Friedrich lowered his head. His neck was prepared for the blow. The clock-punch bit. His card was stamped: arrived for work at such and such a time.

Doomed, doomed! The guardian of the lamps and no living being anymore. Stories of lighting the dead: And Death led him into a room, and in that room there burned myriads upon myriads of lights, and Death spoke, "These you see burning here are the lights of all men's lives, and this one is yours," and it was still strong, but as Death breathed it flickered, and when He stood near it, it seemed about to go out. Friedrich wandered through the ranks of burning bulbs. There, one had gone out. He unscrewed it from its socket, carefully, and wrote down: "Perished during the first minute of the night watch."

It could quite easily go on forever, the night seemed unending, and he took longer and longer routes through the lights, and gave names to the flames: This one is Sibylle, this one is me, this is Beck, that one is famous Walter, and whichever one of us is left gets to keep Sibylle. At which point Sibylle went out.

He reacted like a wild animal, not that he was cruel, but he responded in the simplest, most natural way. He reeled, and caught hold of something: She will die young, she is predestined to die young, and sympathy, and love [and a kind of charity that he would have found repulsive if he'd had his wits about him], and every wish to hasten to her, to swaddle her in blankets, to warm her, to feed and stroke her and kiss her, and protect her with his own body—Oh, your face, your breath, your faint little heartbeat under my chest. There was too much, too much reeling; and he couldn't catch himself. He fell, and striking the circuit rail as he did so, and breaking the next bulb, he caught an electric shock and a burn, and after a rain of spurting light that poured out of the fuse switches like the ultimate firework of a gala evening, it grew dark around him.

In the meantime, what had happened with Sibylle was this: She had waited. She too had heard the door being pulled shut. She too guessed that the door would not open again, a territory had been walled off, in which she would not set foot, and yet she didn't understand any more than Friedrich that her life would not take this direction. She waited. She thought: He's gone out to get something. Then she looked for the telephone. He didn't have a telephone, though; otherwise, she would have called the factory. [Later on, when not even that would help him anymore, he kept a telephone always on the alert, and lived in dread of the rising expense.] It was never ascertained, and maybe she was never in a position to give information about what she purposed in Friedrich's poor room, what she wanted, and how she finally was converted from it. She went foraging, she opened drawers and files, browsed in letters and notes, leafed through books, finally scattered everything that had writing on it round about her, stacked the two chairs in a pyramid arrangement on the table, pulled down the curtain ropes and wove them into a net over the bedposts, and then she left a message, written in block capitals: WHEN THE GOOD GIRL COMES, YOU'RE NEVER HOME! And underneath that, she drew a bold illustration of a little girl going for a walk with a tiger. She attached the board on top of Friedrich's bed, and she left the room.

Yes, she was gone out of the room, and Friedrich, having experienced the miracle of being allowed to remain alive after he had fallen against the live copper circuitry, was carried into his room by an ambulance man. That morning, he lacked tears with which to cry. Not on account of his injuries, a few burns on his left arm, but more the sight of his room where, as he had dreamt, she ought now to have been swinging, high up on the pyramid of chairs on the table, but most especially on account of Beck, who returned to see him, and reported to him on the experiences the pair had had together during the past night.

"Let's go eat," Sibylle had said to him, and they had gone to a wine bar, and then on to other bars, to *palais de danse* that stretched out their tentacular lights into the night, and then to Auntie Molly's, an establishment of which Beck could not say enough, how numerous the women there had been, and how beautiful, and how difficult it had been to get him in. It wasn't just any old bar, oh no! A sign—PRIVATE FUNCTION—had hung on the door, and it had taken Sibylle, who had been received there like an infanta on her birthday, graciously mingling with the common people, to vouch for him to gain him admission. Oh, the folly of youth. Beck was beaming, in spite of the unhappiness that had befallen him later that evening, and Friedrich too felt repulsed by the words, and felt he had been there in these places with their gaudy bottles, their garish film placards, the bartenders with their impassive Prince of Wales faces, the girls with their bare backs, Friedrich too felt firmly convinced [oh, folly of youth!] that the delight of life had been tasted, the height, the zenith, apogee with Sibylle, what an apotheosis for Beck! No fairy came to Friedrich to console him. Not to any of the young men who stand in the doorways shivering in the biting evening wind, listening to the music that floats out on to the street, does she come and help. It's a shame, because that would be a simple and grateful and also a natural task for a fairy. She would only have to lift up a corner of the curtain, open the door a crack, make a wall transparent, and say: "Don't be sad, here, look, it's nothing special; just one of those funny masks people wear over their fear of life, listen to their hearts, press your ear against the chest of that blissful-looking fellow, do it the way a doctor does it, put on a serious expression, and do you feel the heart beating so feebly, so dully, so without any hope for happiness, like the trot of a heavy cab horse going home late at night, at the end of a long day's waiting outside the drafty cavernous hole of the station hall?" No fairy had come out to him, and so it happened that that morning Friedrich [it was a miracle, remember, that he was alive] had to suffer from a foolish, silly superficiality that need hardly have concerned him. And then when Beck suddenly started yelling and jumping up and down in front of Friedrich's bed again, and had obviously gone completely mad, suddenly claiming Sibylle loved him, loved Friedrich, and that she must have run off to him out of Auntie Molly's [famous, as we know, on account of the scandalous relationships among prominent people that were said to flourish there]—at that, Friedrich thought: No, she doesn't love me, she will never come to me again. But externally, toward Beck, he was careful to laugh, or at least he tried to, he twisted his mouth a little, he stuck the tip of his tongue out between his teeth, he made his mouth a little pointed, open, catlike, ambiguous, he thought, in the hope that Beck would hurl himself at him, and they would have a wrestling match.

A Sad Affair

THE DAY had risen. Across the bleached foggy horizon—contrasting with it in color and fixity—lay the window bars in front of the window of Friedrich's room in the Grand Hotel of the foreign city. The noise in the corridor had increased. Pale, morning hands pulled the shoes inside from the doorstep. *Thou shouldest wear sandals on thy feet!* The man, the guest, the resident, was getting ready. The breakfast symphony sounded through the building. Clatter of dishes, knives, spoons, and cups. In the walls, the bathwater was going up and down; powerful and pure, it streamed into the tubs, scummy and discolored it gurgled away again into deep subterranean channels, taking with it the dust from the bodies of a traveling humanity, into the network of pipes under the city, and thence to never-seen sewage fields. Time had marched on, the minute hand had been once round, and Friedrich was still lying in the knotted sheets on his rumpled bed, and it was surprising in more than one way that he was still there. He was in the great city, where he had wanted to be. He had only to get up and go, and Sibylle would be there, visible to his eyes and palpable to his hands. His wish had been fulfilled, his longing could be satisfied. Why then was he still hesitating? Was he like an ancient clipper ship that, having found peace in the harbor, trembles with desire in the ropes of its rigging when the wind blows the salt breath of the sea to it, and yet, for all its longing, creaks and aches in every spar when happiness sets its sails, weighs its anchor, and sets its course for the great breakers? Was he past that? Not in terms of years. But possibly he was used up, the flame had already consumed his being, his sensibility, and his heart; and was he so exhausted with it, gone cold and weak, that he hadn't even noticed that in him there was just an orange core of warmth in a pile of ashes? The game had been played and lost a hundred times. Opinions differed on the way he had taken defeat. Some said he was on the run from guilt, because they reckoned a man in his situation, after so many and such public reversals, had no option but to pay with his life. Beck, who had left the fray and embarked on a new liaison [Sibylle had not been destined for him!] but kept an eye on developments, would reply to them: "But he is paying, look at the life he's living." And Friedrich himself remained entangled in the inevitable conclusion of all his thinking: *She is destined for me! I will one day prevail.* Perhaps he was a gambler. We like to seek out the banal and otherworldly explanation, and are afraid to say: "He had been chosen by Fate [the devilish or demonic, but always, one way or another, the destructive force] to love this one among all the women in the world."

He stood in front of the door of the St. Peter's Hostel, and was five minutes late. He had taken a cab to ease his journey. To take the weight off his feet. To be able to bound up the steps. Once, she had said to him: "You don't love me at all, that's just an illusion; but you love the idea of being in love with me!" He knocked on the door and opened it and knew, when he saw her lying in an iron bed crowded with toys, black dogs and brown bears, still sleepy, pink, dreamy, rubbing her eyes, looking up and then stretching out her hand, the smell of her perfume, "After the Storm," in the room, and the smell of her, Sibyllesmell, the aroma he had once whimpered to dwell in [in one of his letters to her, he had written: "In the Northland, in the upper reaches of the Baltic, where lonely pines rise out of the tundra, and beckon to your sisters in the white nights of June, where reindeer graze, unsaddled and unmilked by men, the air is so pure in the soft drift of the summer breeze that it must be like the coming and going of your sleeping breath, Sibylle"], and he knew that the accusation about being in love with love was nonsense. He would so have liked to say: "Little Sibylle," and sit down on her bed, but that wasn't possible, that didn't accord with the protocol that had established itself between them, and which broadly he respected.

"Will you go and get me some breakfast?" she asked, and he went downstairs to the dining room, and there, at the buffet, softly [because, while he enjoyed serving others, being served made him bashful] asked for breakfast for the lady in room fourteen. And while he was standing at the buffet waiting, and watching the maid disappear into the kitchen with his order, his eyes, for once raised up, happened to light upon a sign over the cupboard where the bottles were kept, a dusty, smoked sign that read in old-fashioned signwriting: ST. PETER'S HOSTEL, DOCTOR MAGNUS FOUNDATION FOR REFUGEES OF ALL NATIONS.

What was this, what did that signify: "Doctor Magnus Foundation for Refugees of All Nations"? Was Sibylle a refugee? Hardly. But then why was she sleeping in a hostel for refugees? Anyway, what refugees, and who was this Doctor Magnus that he felt able to take them in? The simplest explanation was that this was merely an old sign, a pub sign, a bit of the history of the hostel, and without any relevance to today, kept out of piety and respect, and hung up over the cupboard of wines and essences and brandies. That must be it, in the Wild Man Pub, you hardly expected to run into the wild man in person. And yet, Friedrich felt vaguely disquieted by the sign. Moved by the sleepy face of his beloved, he had been on his way back to her, to resume their old game, a man who is happy if his humble, loving gift is accepted. Now experience called on him to "Beware." What new traps were lying open for him? He was ready to tie the mask on tighter, to play the traveler passing through, merely by chance, with no particular interest. As he turned to go back upstairs to Sibylle's room, he saw Anja. She stood behind him, she must have crept into the room like an animal on velvet paws. Night hadn't changed her. She was unkempt and didn't seem to have taken off her clothes. The shaggy sheepskin hung off her just as heavily as it had the previous evening. Even the cigarette she was drawing on hurriedly and impatiently, blowing the smoke up to the ceiling in blue rings, might be the same as yesterday's, though in all probability there had been dozens of others in between. So other members of the troupe than just Sibylle and Fedor were staying at St. Peter's. Perhaps it was cheap, and well known to groups of traveling artists. That could easily be the explanation. The sight of Anja had the effect of calming Friedrich's nerves a little. He still didn't know how to greet her, though—Anja, the clown of the troupe, the girl with the soft features and the red mouth. He was shy of being too intimate with people he didn't really know, even if he happened to have bumped into them once already. He contented himself with nodding to her, to show that he knew who she was, and going on by.

In her room, Sibylle had wrapped herself in a dressing gown and was pacing up and down. It was her tiger walk, as Friedrich called it, a taut, nervous, springy gait. It was a sign that she was thinking, that she was intellectually occupied, invariably hunting for some argument that would bolster her current position, whatever it was. Like Anja, she was smoking in short, swift, vehement puffs. These girls, thought Friedrich, they're under pressure, under pressure from something that sets them apart from the world. "I've ordered breakfast," he said, "and Anja's downstairs, smoking like you. I think of her in her sheepskin as a young refugee, pacing up and down next to her tired horse and her heavily laden cart."

Sibylle straightway got excited: "I don't want you to say anything against Anja [had he done such a thing?], I like her, she's the daughter of a prince, and when she was a child, a babe in arms, she saw Moscow burning." That could very well be, why not, Friedrich was quite used to the Russians that you met in Europe being descended from princes, and even the thing about Moscow burning could perfectly well be true. A little émigrée, in other words. Someone without a will of her own, flotsam. If it came down to it, weren't they all children of the War? He had often thought about that in the time he'd been away from Sibylle. He looked back on the day when the world had been supposed to end. Prophets had come forth all over the land, predicting it. Their words had sprouted like weeds on the farms and in the towns and villages along the Polish frontier. There were smallholders who had sold up, turned everything into cash, and hastened to the bars, to enjoy the end of their time with drinking and eating and whoring—because what better was there to do in their fear of the end, if they weren't to huddle together in prayer like toothless old women? Fires were blazing wherever you looked, along the banks of the Vistula and on the rafts. The bargemen got drunk and so did the peasants. The

farmers and the craftsmen. The flat white caps of the Russian
Imperial borderers sailed into the air, in pursuit of the elusive spirit
of vodka, while they—Friedrich could picture the scene to himself
as if he had dreamed it yesterday, even though he had been no
more than six years old on the day the world had ended—his
mother [the faint whiff of Leichner powder on her face], himself,
and that nice, slender, colorful lieutenant, Uncle Thomas from the
Uhlans, had stood on the balcony of their house to watch
Friedrich's father go up in a balloon from the field behind the gas-
works to greet the comet that was coming to destroy the world. It
was truly a heroic act, comparable to the flight of Icarus, magnificent, the desire to cut loose from the Earth now trembling in panic,
and to steer a course straight for perdition, toward the fixed star,
into the arms of the lethal light. But that was typical of Friedrich's
father. He would confront the demons! Who said the prophets
were mistaken? And people in the Middle Ages were cleverer than
we were, when they blocked off their wells and led their animals
into the darkness of the light-garlanded stables and sheds at the
approach of the trailing light in the night sky, because God did not
want any yellow silk gas balloons floating toward the sign He had
made in the air, and God knocked them to the ground. The people
on the balcony, and all the others who were watching from the
ground, saw the balloon rising higher and higher until it was just a
dot among the stars, and then the comet came, and then came a
fall, something, something indiscernible that plummeted down,
and then a gasp from many voices, repeated, and the wreckage
came down exactly on the frontier with Poland. On the night that
Friedrich lost his father, on that night of the comet, in another part

of the country, in the heart of a different landscape, Sibylle was born. Who could blame Friedrich for turning this death and this birth [when, already in love with her, he first learned of her] into the work of a fate to which he could not pray but could at least raise his hands toward in rage and in supplication? Had the comet not been a sign, a flaming sword? Uncle Thomas, the short, slender, jolly lieutenant in the Uhlans, lay buried in the Masurian forests. Friedrich had seen his grave, a little hump on the ground, marked by a propeller; the lieutenant had met his death as a fighter pilot. Friedrich's mother had collapsed after gleaning potatoes in a field that hadn't wanted to bear any more in 1918; the faint scent of the layer of stage powder from the yellow box and the feeling of her bony hands were all the memories of her that were left him. He thought of the long walks for milk in the early, black winter afternoons in the east, where you had to go for miles to the nearest ruined outbuildings, up to your knees in snow, sometimes stopping to listen whether it was the wolf coming after you. And he thought that, in another form, Sibylle must have had the same youth, standing in line for a little bit of butter at bare brick dairies in a gaggle of feeble women whose nerves would feel fear—yes, but not their hearts, which had grown impervious—when the drone of an airplane made them think a bomb was coming. And Anja too, if he wanted to adopt her into his Holy Family [for which there was every reason], Anja had seen Moscow, in flames, or some other town on the Volga, and at a time when she'd been quiet and dreamy still, the daughter of a prince! [oh, castles and estates with extensive gallops, with sleigh rides across the snow fields in the little light of the lamp attached to the pole between the two horses' heads, and the brilliance of the celebrations in the Kremlin, the young ladies wrapped in Brussels lace with lit candles in their hands], lying in her crib, which was the arms of a nurse who had fled with her, loyal and in disguise and in the hay of a cart belonging to a distiller from the edge of town. Eyes peeped through their lashes after sleep, and the whole sky was red, and the little girl stretched out her little arms toward the brilliance and, in rapture at the turning world, said: *"Da!"*

Now and again, Sibylle would interrupt her pacing. She did so suddenly, and with unusual violence. She tossed away the end of her cigarette, crushed it underfoot like a man, and said: "Oh, you don't need to know any of that, really." Had she turned cowardly? She had taken a long run-up to an explanation, had wanted to speak, and now she was hesitating, behaving like a cat on a hot, as the proverb says, tin roof. She climbed back into bed [was it to drive off? She knew the game: a bed is a car, beepbeep, gangway] and balanced the breakfast tray, which had arrived, on her knees, which she had drawn up to her chest. Friedrich stood with his back to the window to watch her. The thought that she might have become a coward, full of subterfuges and secrets and not the courage to speak, now alarmed him. That, if that were indeed the case, would be a different Sibylle. She had never made a secret of anything, and had always owned up to whatever she had done. There was no Sibylle of lies. On the street in summer in bright sunshine, she might well try to persuade you: "We need to put up our umbrellas and buy new winter coats, it's snowing," but never did a lie that was not obviously a lie [for love of lying] spring from her lips. She had never used untruths or strategic evasions to gain a small, momentary advantage. Had that changed now, was she on the slippery slope, with herself no longer firmly in grip? Friedrich felt doubtful. Her face no longer had the tranquillity of the good girl. It was excited and looked somehow scraped, the face of a scout. Sharper in its lines and angles too. Was she looking straight ahead? Could she still steer her life, careful of every stone that might knock it off its course? Friedrich didn't know. He couldn't tell. As ever when he was confronted with Sibylle, he regretted that he wasn't a clairvoyant. What was going on behind her brow? It was a fortress, a bulwark, a concrete wall that kept repulsing him. If only he could manage to penetrate the windings of her brain, even once! That must be the key. He suffered from highly specific fantasies and saw an immaterial action as concretely as a blueprint in an educational film. He watched his thinking climb out of his head into hers, and he followed it, as like a red arrow it followed the mazy white tracks of her ponderings. He was palping the most sensitive nerves of her being. He wanted to know them. He wanted to find out: What am I to her, what is she thinking, where is salvation, can I right her and steer her [her misunderstanding!], and win her and make everything turn out well? What he wished to accomplish was a crime; the worst crime possible: to break into another's soul. But that's how it was between them. He was unable to withstand his desire to feel with her. So he was only thinking, as she always said, of himself and his own happiness. Maybe this thinking, this demented desire to possess that went far beyond the merely physical, was the reason why she refused to surrender her life to his claims, because his demands were too steep and too strange and caused a shudder to pass across her back. But: was he truly strange

to her? It was to ascertain this, precisely this, that he was compelled
to wish for a magical diving suit, his secret burglar's clothing, the
devilish plan, to be able to inveigle himself into the chambers of
her being. There she was, sitting in front of him, sipping tea in bed,
and biting off a piece of croissant, and getting her mouth all jammy.
What was her spell, why didn't he go, take his hat and pay the bill
at the ridiculous hotel on the lake that wasn't his style, and travel on
to the places listed on the ticket in his pocket? What was her spell?
Was she beautiful, or rather, was she still beautiful? Friedrich
remembered passing through the revolving doors of a café once,
and, seeing her coming down from the upper story, so transcen-
dently beautiful, so angelically delicate that he had to close his eyes
lest they be blinded by such light, while a sea of tears—as deep as
the tropical sea after the sun has gone down, and the forest
breathes cinnamon, and cougars scream as they stare from waving
palm fronds into the illimitable mirror—while a sea, then, of tears,
a sweet ocean of happiness and emotion, fell from the bed of his
closed eyes into his heart, splashy and soothing, so that it felt like
dying, unconsciousness, sinking, subsiding, the death of a child of
god that had seen her. That was how beautiful she was. And so
young. A blue dragoon's coat with gray braid set off her face: head
of Eros against idyllic Aegean backdrop. Now, for the last time, was
she still as beautiful? He was able to behold her, so was the dazzling
magic gone, and could he go? No! He loved her. Nothing changed.
He was entranced. The longer he looked at her, the more profoundly he felt tied. She put the tray down on the ground, made a
deliberate effort, and said: "So do you not like Fedor?"

A difficult question. He had to be careful not to offend her. He replied [and once more his heart was in the grip of another's hand]: "I hardly know him." And then, as the silence thickened in the room, and to take a little of the importance out of the subject (which irked him), he added: "I'm sorry, I'm not really interested in Fedor. I assume you've become friends, which I can understand in the situation you're both in, but I'm sure it'll pass."

To which she nodded, and said: "It's so stupid, you know he's like a child."

Friedrich was aghast when he heard that. An abyss opened at his feet. It was what he'd been terrified of. But he didn't want to jump into it. Not yet. He struggled for the self-mastery of the indifferent traveler, the man merely passing through. He said: "Well, never mind, that's not what's important," which was pretty stupid of him; and then came another question, in a voice that tried to mask the fact that it was shaking and slightly deranged: "And who do you love?"

"Who do I love? How can you ask?" She looked earnest and sure of herself and perhaps a little indignant: "I only love Bosporus, you know that!"

Friedrich made a feeble gesture of agreement and recognition. Bosporus was an officer who had been with the German troops in Turkey, and following the armistice, as they were returning through the Ukraine, had had his knee shattered by a bullet while he was perched on front of the locomotive, his rifle ready. "What about Doctor Magnus?" This question wasn't from Friedrich, it was just his voice, which had made itself independent of him, and to his own horror, put such a question.

"Magnus? I'm fond of him."

At that moment, there was a knock, and Fedor walked in. Friedrich had difficulty concealing his astonishment. So there was a Doctor Magnus, he must be alive for Sibylle to be fond of him, the plaque in the dining room over the buffet was more than just some dusty relic, this foundation for refugees from all countries, and this house, there was something in it, it was alchemy, and he, as if he hadn't sensed it already, had blundered into it! Fedor too was unchanged from the previous evening. He was in his sweater, as though determined he would greet the world always just like that. He kissed Sibylle's hand and shook Friedrich's firmly, like a friend. "How did you sleep?"

The question was directed at Friedrich, and Friedrich nodded: "Fine." What else was he supposed to say? Fedor simply expected that Friedrich would have slept well, that was a given, it was really the least you could expect if someone was staying at the Grand Hotel on the lake. Fedor was doing turns. He climbed onto the bedframe and balanced on top of it. Quite agile, but Friedrich thought: What do I do if he falls on to the bed? He wondered whether he would be able to endure that. But Fedor didn't fall, he vaulted back on the floor, and opened a little box of chocolates on the bedside table.

"They're from Magnus," said Sibylle. It was a request to him not to touch them. But Fedor was unable to hear that. He was insouciant [Sibylle called him naive] and he stuffed his mouth full of chocolates, and then he offered the box to Friedrich. Friedrich didn't feel like chocolate, but he didn't want to admit to himself that he was furious with Fedor for having failed to understand Sibylle's unspoken request; he helped himself to some of the chocolates, to make himself Fedor's accomplice. "You're behaving like swine," she screamed.

Fedor looked amazed: "What do you mean?"

Friedrich knew, and he felt sorry for Sibylle. It wasn't the chocolates, it was the breach of her prerogative that offended her. She always lived ringed by invisible pastures where no one was allowed to set foot. Why not do her the kindness, and agree to respect her boundaries? And, for the second time that morning, Friedrich felt like saying: "Little Sibylle."

But she had had enough of being at a physical disadvantage, the person lying in bed among others upright and dressed, and brusquely she leaped out of bed—making any feeling of tenderness quite inappropriate—ran over to the bathtub, turned on the faucets, supplementing the water with mixtures from mysterious bottles, was as enigmatically industrious as an apothecary or even an alchemist, and finally immersed herself completely, head and all, into the brimming water, and seemed not to want to come out of it, as if she were proposing to drown herself. Then she got dressed, little culottes, no top, powdered herself, wiped about her eyes, all with an animal agreeableness and naturalness and deliberateness, and when there was another, and this time a quieter, knock on the door, she called out: "Come in." It was Anja in her sheepskin.

With the entrance of this creature—this dreamy prince's daughter and clown of the troupe, soft mouth sucking rapidly and greedily on a cigarette—Sibylle transformed herself into a cavalier. She was as courtly as a well-brought-up young man from a prime regiment—no loutish heel-clack, but the soft, coaxing hand of an authentic gentleman, in whom politeness has softened into near-casualness—as she made room for Anja on her hurriedly made bed. So she was still that, a cavalier! Friedrich noted it happily. He knew that it was part of her manner, which he loved, to be courteous, friendly, and kind, to be solicitous to the few girls she allowed to come near her [she was more usually surrounded by men, but a girlfriend had been her dream from childhood on], just as a good rider flatters his horse and, with the respect he shows it, ennobles himself even as he tells it how to trot; and none of it done expressly or with any intention.

Fedor appeared oblivious of the style, the tone that prevailed between the girls. He tossed everything into one pan and assumed that whatever he ate from it must be good. And so he now proceeded to suggest a meal together in a restaurant that belonged to an organization and was supposed to be inexpensive. Friedrich saw Sibylle slipping away from him, lost to him all this day, he was fumbling for an excuse not to go to this organization restaurant, which seemed repugnant to him before he'd even seen it, but Sibylle had already taken the initiative and said "No." "No, Friedrich is only here for today, and he and I need to talk. Now run along and leave us alone."

That rough form of rejection was awkward for Friedrich. He would gladly have taken the edge off it with a word or two, perhaps an invitation for later on. He thought Fedor would blush and be furious. But all he did was laugh, and laughing, say: "You and your secrets!" And he walked over to Sibylle, kissed her on the forehead [she allowed it to happen; therefore, it was allowed], tried to put his arm round Anja too, but she pushed it aside, and went out, already humming to himself. He really was, as Sibylle called him, an uncomplicated fellow. Just a boy, thought Friedrich, it's too bad that I can't be equally nice and open and chirpy in my dealings with him. But there was the poison on Friedrich's side that got in the way of any friendly feelings he might have toward Fedor, the poison that had corrupted and tainted his soul, his body, his being such as it was from its very foundations: Fedor is one of those people who has the apple of felicity land in their lap, without having to go to any trouble to pluck it, he is one of those who wake up in the morning holding the diamond in their hands, one of those who don't understand what is being done to them, he is the man, one of the men, but they are a type, a species, the man for whom Sibylle is not intended, and [oh, unaccountable world!] still he holds her, even if he doesn't realize who it is [in his arms]. Wasn't Friedrich therefore bound to hate Fedor? Wasn't it natural that he thought the cloud is lifting, the day will be fine, when the door closed behind him?

Sibylle had sent Fedor away in order to remain alone with Friedrich. She, who hated writing letters, had, since she'd been living abroad, to his delight sent him letters regularly, sometimes quite long and detailed. Reading between the lines of the last of them, Friedrich had thought he took a "Won't you come visit?" and a violent confusion. He was right about both. Her handwriting, her large, solid, upright, almost printed roman hand had gone astray. The verticals no longer went so steeply up. The trunks of the letters seemed broken, and a shrill nervousness beetled madly across the pages in the guise of a wild scatter of dots, and of bizarrely twisted and contorted lines. These were letters that made Friedrich wildly agitated when they reached him. He replied with telegrams and screeds of his own, sent declarations of love, marriage proposals, offers of shared apartments, lengthy explanations, detailed news, desperate beseechings, and a thousand good wishes, out into the world, all bundled together into one long "Come back!" He hurried to train stations, to airfields, to telephone exchanges in order to be able to reach her promptly and immediately.

To Sibylle, he was a shadow. Her eyes barely took him in as a physical shape. He might stand before her, as now, or he might be far away from her in a different country—it made no difference, he was still a shadow. He was a piece of her past, a thing in her present, and whether he would be an item in her future, that remained to be seen. The shadow didn't offend her eyes, it could camouflage itself like a chameleon—since, in her eyes, he always seemed to take on the shade of the wallpaper, he was even a little less than gray, he was of a tonelessly discreet appearance. This had not always been the case. She had seen him once. At first even seen straight through him [as she thought] with terror and inexplicable desire. Then he had been a flame, a human torch, consuming itself. She thought of the Christians in the gardens of the Emperor Nero. Her terror had eaten up her [inexplicable, in any case] desire. He had turned into a vision, hurrying toward her through the myriad streets of the megalopolis. She would dream of him at night. Every owl's flutter outside her fifth-floor window was his ghostly knocking. She stopped sleeping at home. He was the reason that she went off to sleep away, he caused her to ask Beck to keep watch over her at night, it was Friedrich, who never took his eyes off her life. He was always ready. Running up like a sprinter. Breathless, pale, a pounding in his neck. To him it was like running for his life. Maybe like running for her life. No one knew which, back then.

She played along, put on a brave face, sometimes asking herself, vulgarly, in the coarse women's expression: "Is this the Devil in me?" He thought so anyway, Beck thought so, everyone thought so; later on, even Bosporus would think so. It was unquestionably a relationship. She called him up in the morning, once she'd dared to return home, called him up and asked him to come over, to put on some milk for her while she was resting, beat her an egg, read to her from one of the books that lay around her bed in great piles. Each time she called, she heard the way he plucked the receiver off the cradle at the first hint of a ring, snatched up by a hand that had lain in vigil during a sleepless night: *She's going to call me.* And no sooner was the conversation over than he was already there, standing in front of her in her room, a runner, bending down over her, breathless, pale, a pounding in his neck. He really had come at a run; he had no money at that time, no money at all, he was dirt-poor and he ran great distances, his knees thrown up, his hair flapping, the lover running amok, charging blindly into pedestrians on the street and spilling them into the gutter. There was something terrifying about him, which she felt, while others merely shuddered involuntarily.

Once, she was ill; Friedrich didn't leave her bedside, he tended her, washed her things, cooked her meals, shook the pillows, read her stories, playacted the lame man, and gave performances of exotic gentlemen, the Marquis of Oyakahoma desires to lay his country's celebrated moon at the feet of the sick princess, he juggled with balls, something he was only able to do in the rapture of his passion; all of it done to delight her heart, and when she laughed, he felt like a field full of larks taking wing in the morning;

but the doctor, old Doctor Rapp, a friend of hers, said, when Friedrich passed him something: "Why are your hands shaking? You look like someone who's had the skin peeled from his face, who's suffering agonies of fever and fire." He had reached such a pass. She had hated him when it became clear, when she noticed. She had hated him, because, having come so far, in the hours when he was all done up, the prepared sacrificial victim, because like a dead beast he represented a seduction to her, in spite of her will and her judgment. Then she would feel herself driven, with the full horror of a forced woman, to do his every bidding. But not once had he taken advantage of such a situation. Was he too busy running into the walls with his head, the walls of the prison he thought he was caught in, the invisible walls that kept moving nearer together, that were already a cell as fitted as a corset and kept him from breathing? Or was it insane arrogance that kept him from exploiting a tailor-made situation and taking her?

Beck had told him once, and Sibylle knew it: "Take her, why don't you, take her, she wants to be taken; like this, you're just going to the dogs, and Sibylle's going to the dogs, make an end and take her!"

To which Friedrich—a fool hanging from a silken thread over an abyss—had replied: "Please understand me, Beck. I'm not after some shabby transaction. I love Sibylle; it's quite impossible for me to touch her, even against the appearance of her will."

And Sibylle had got to hear of this as well. So he wanted a consummation in happiness and joy. Maybe he dreamed she would come to him. Probably he did. And why didn't she? She had never come up with an answer to that. It never happened, that was all.

She too could feel the invisible wall he kept running into. Once, it was before Christmas, and she had to take the early train home to her parents, by the river, he had [she needed someone, to wake her, to fix her breakfast] stayed the night with her. It was a night they had both been happy, like children. She had liked it and [though not saying anything] been surprised by it. Liked it so much that, no sooner back in the city, she had repeated the experiment. With the same result. But then that too had palled. It got so that she had said to him: "All right, stay if you like, but I want you to know I love Bosporus [that time had already started] and you'll have to lie with me like old Socrates did with young Alcibiades." He passed the test. His heart had beat happily and vigorously. There was a joy in him: *I am lying beside Sibylle!* She told him stories about what she'd been like as a child and a schoolgirl, how her father [a poet and a Buddhist and a manufacturer of plaster angels for Catholic countries, exports to Latin America] had introduced her to literature, at thirteen to Schopenhauer and Nietzsche and George, Stendhal and Baudelaire, and how, indiscriminately, as a child she had made her way through libraries to the books of the mystics [spent days lounging in bed!], and then, arrived in the capital city, she had been inducted in matters of love by the celebrated critic Walter in Frühling's well-known brothel [a little bird with open eyes: but that's the way of the world!]. It had been very pleasant, to be talking with Friedrich in one bed together, warmed by one blanket. Thereupon she had fallen asleep, and Friedrich had guarded her sleep until she had started crying brokenheartedly in her dream, sobbing deeply, utterly, utterly miserable, like young kittens taken away from their mother, and when she woke up with a cry and started lashing out, then Friedrich thought she must have been dreaming that he, as had not been the case, had left the role of the old Socrates. He was crushed. That was the blow that ruined this night [which he, in his hubris had called—oh, folly of youth—the loveliest of his life] and filled him with grief and rage and illimitable despair and every kind of blasphemy.

Sibylle had felt it: So this is what he thinks now. She had known it. Now might have been the moment to surprise him. She might have lent him wings. The only reason she had been crying was because they had killed her favorite cuddly toy, Volleyball, a black dog. She had the magic in her hands, all she had needed to say would have been: "Change, old Socrates, abracadabra, to Alcibiades." But she had pronounced no spell, no word had passed her lips, she had turned her face to the wall, and murmured: "It's late, go to sleep." Nothing had transpired, then or at any other time, the invisible wall between them was intact. And then Friedrich had turned gray, or had begun to take on the varying but always pallid hues of the wallpaper behind him; to put it another way, they had both become tired, Nature had exhausted herself in them, she wasn't capable of producing the same measure of terror again and again in all perpetuity, and so all that remained had been this: Friedrich loved her, she was able to rely on him and his love; and what good did that do? Only her leaving the country had given him a little new interest. She was in turmoil, and he represented home, represented the city she loved, she wanted to talk to him, she wanted him to keep her informed, maybe she wanted to go home, but it was difficult to begin explaining the particular circumstances to him in which she found herself.

Anja had not quit the place on Sibylle's bed that Sibylle had cleared for her. She was still leaning against the pillows, puffing blue-gray cigarette smoke into the air, which under the ceiling was already heavy and dark, a cloudy seraglio sky. Anja was unimaginable without tobacco smoke. It was part of her nature, the ambience in which she lived, the tent she put up around her. She was always at home, always *chez soi*, wherever she happened to be sojourning, and it sometimes happened that her chance temporary hosts came to her to say good-bye: "Unfortunately, we have to go, but thank you, we very much enjoyed our stay with you"; so much more real than any room or apartment was Anja's castle in the air, so solidly put together from the misty blue rings of hastily drained cigarettes. When Sibylle had finished dressing, finished getting ready, thrown on her coat, put on her cap, and was on the point of leaving the room with Friedrich, Anja turned to Sibylle and said: "Magnus wants to see you."

Sibylle made a vague, dismissive gesture: "Later, maybe this evening, in the theater," and Anja was left in sole possession of her realm.

"Magnus is her husband," Sibylle said when they were on the street. They were walking through a district of ugly, plain, modern buildings. Leafless poplars withered at fifteen-pace intervals in the little squares cut out of the edge of the pavement showing the soil below, and their boughs looked like the hands of desperate, half-crazy people flung out above their heads and begging. A keen wind blew straight down the street. "That's a glacier wind from the mountains," Sibylle spoke into the wind. "When we get to the lake, you'll be able to see the white peaks in the distance."

They needed to lean forward like bicyclists pushing on the pedals with all their force, so as not to be thrown backward. On the corners, cross-breezes pulled aside Sibylle's coattails and picked up her skirts. Her bare, frost-reddened knees appeared momentarily. She's still the little girl in short socks, he thought, my plucky companion. He put his arm around her shoulder; she let it happen. He was once more moved, and both of them [for different reasons] were awkward. To him, her bare, scabbed knees were an embodiment of Sibylle's decency. They made it easier to be him. "She's a boy," he said to himself [he had said it many times], "a boy that I can treat like a young friend of mine." In fact, though, it was precisely in these moments when he pushed her girl nature into a different, unspecified, and, he thought, an asexual, if still erotic, role that his desire to call Sibylle his own (*she is destined to be mine!*) was especially acute and urgent, stabbing him with sharp needles from the hair on his head to the tips of his toes. He was also like the sculptor in front of his own statue. He saw her as a good piece of work, a successful endeavor, felt she was an incarnation of the concept *body*, firm and claspable, perhaps even asking to be picked up off the ground and held. "I am the Atlas who carries you, and you are a star for me, untouched in space, touched only by my arm which is your support." He would have liked to say that to her. With his arm on her shoulder, he clasped her and enfolded her entire being in a wide, protective embrace.

And because she too had the sensation that she was being contained (He's wrapping me up, he's carrying me, warming me), she freed herself of the weight of his arm with a sudden jerk, an abrupt spinning free of her form, a quick twitch of the mouth, and when she saw that he was upset, and since she knew the truth of his affection for her, she produced herself in gross insults, words that frightened her, once they had come out of her mouth and made a sound in air. "You're like a toad, you're like a toad crawling on my back, a slimy scaly goggle-eyed toad in a swamp!"—and the evocation terrified and disgusted them.

The world bucked him. There was no reason and no sense in it, it was incomprehensible. He was not allowed to touch her. Strangers, people on the street, all comers practically, were allowed to hold her. The rending wolf's bites that had torn his heart when he had seen at a party in the capital how extras in tails with little brilliantined Hollywood mustaches had touched her lips with theirs. "Oh, that's completely harmless, a kiss at a party, don't be silly," she had said. And she was right, of course, it was silly to get excited, but was it not the cry of the man dying of thirst in the desert that had broken from him, terrible, cracked, almost rabid in its shame and despair? Her lips seemed to him the font of life, the source of all joys, the world offered no drink to set beside the kiss of her lips and never, never once, had he been allowed to breathe on them, to feel them, their redness, their flesh, their moist gleam that shone to his faint spirit, a craving, a signal, a finishing line in a gauntlet race through an infernal landscape, to the scornful laughter of the happy, the contented, the sated, the living; he was without anyone to pity him, the compassion of the world denied itself to him with these same lips. They walked awkwardly on, calamity shielded them, evil spirits danced in the wind, they were two convicts chained together, attempting to flee but about to be caught, they walked faster.

Sibylle had been glad too. "He's coming, good, I want him to stay." Friedrich's desire to stay had been Sibylle's desire too. And yet the impossibility, the impracticability of this desire had struck them both in the very second they had seen one another again. It was glaring; there was no point in even talking about it. There was nothing to be done about it, it just wouldn't go. The invisible wall rose up, you left of the wall, me right of the wall, that's the way it is, the wall between us remains intact. When they respected that border, and looked at each other like objects in a shop window, then they could be one heart and one soul.

It is a mistake to think they were joyless. The little joys of the day were there for them. To Friedrich, having choked down the toad, they even seemed enormous. Wasn't he walking with Sibylle, didn't he see her, feel her, couldn't he sometimes [only not too often] bump into her as if by accident and for a split second feel her as something more than imaginary? Was it not bliss that she existed, that she was alive in the world at the same time as he was, and that he had received the blessing of knowing her, of meeting her, of being allowed to walk with her here? Certainly, it was bliss, and he scolded himself for being an ingrate if he complained. When he was away from her, he was sometimes befallen by the sweet giddy notion: She is breathing, somewhere in the world, she is breathing the air. Heart beating, restless and sleepless, tossing on his bed at night, he had felt the pulsing of her blood as well. She is my contemporary! Even that was substantially a source of happiness.

How great was her capacity for joy. Was there anyone in the world who could feel so much joy? He looked at her and felt like doing handsprings. The way her eyes assailed the window displays in the Bahnhofstrasse, which they had now reached. "Hey, look at the scarf with the tiger on it! Will you buy me that tiger scarf? And I've seen some shoes, the sweetest shoes, with really low heels, the kind you like, and made out of the skin of a southwest Indian river mule! Are there such things as river mules? Do they have rivers in southwest India? You've absolutely got to buy me a map so I can find out, I want a wild, garish, luminous map, drawn by ancient sages, checked by stargazers with beards longer than the tower they live in, and with flying crocodiles on it and cannibals, hungry black ones, roasting a fat white missionary. Come on, let's go in this store, it's so posh, I'm sure only marquises come in here otherwise, let's ask them for a bra for two, husband and wife, or one for an entire family. Come on. And will you find out for me what those feather boas cost, I'd so like to wear a feather boa, you know all my life it's been my dream to wear a feather boa, that, and to marry a man with two wooden legs that he locks up in a cage every night so they don't run away; their names are Peter and Paul, you know, like the fortress in Russia, where they killed all those people just because the czar didn't like them, I'm sure you know that, Anja knows it too. Oh, don't be so stupid. You're such a killjoy. I want you to limp now, I want you to drag one leg behind, and to stare straight up into space."

And Friedrich limped, dragging one leg behind, staring straight up into space, and Sibylle laughed until she felt ill, and the people on the street stopped and stared, and Sibylle and Friedrich clasped hands and danced in the middle of everyone, and the people were happy and wore happy smiles, and said: "Ah, what is it to be young," and they remembered, and old men stroked the hands of old women, the air felt somehow a little balmy, a gutter lad sang out: "Love is a many splendored thing," and he drew out the melody longer and longer, and the bicycle he perched on turned with it, easily, sweetly, purringly, just like a wickedly elegant electric Italian hurdy gurdy—and then suddenly Friedrich and Sibylle let go of the other's hand, and stopped dancing and laughing and looked at each other, earnestly and awkwardly, blushing and with mounting indignation [but against what?], and the wind blew harder, and people's expressions changed as they said: "Well, really, grown-ups behaving like silly children, the things these tourists permit themselves in our public streets," and the gutter lad yelled and stamped on his pedal: "Must have been bitten by the wild waddock."

Bitten by the wild waddock? Could be. They stopped to have something to eat. It was late. The restaurant on the shore had already lit its lamps. It might have been anywhere, blandly neutral and characterless in its design. Sibylle ordered salads, lots of fun greenery. Friedrich wanted wine. From the lake terrace, it was still just possible to see the sun on the tips of the mountains. Dark bulks with white snowcaps high in the sky, they constituted the background and the end to the lake. It was on those slopes that the wine had grown in summer, good wine. Friedrich drank it in large, rushed mouthfuls; it was calming. He said: "To you, Sibylle." So there he was, a gentleman in a rich, famous, foreign city, sitting opposite the queen of his heart, and drinking wine from the snow-capped mountains. Was he not to be envied? Who else led such a life, who could boast of doing anything comparable now? And if it should cost him his life, then this hour was worth it. You needed to wear blinders, it wasn't good to see everything; already the lake fogs were brewing up ghosts on the surface of the water and the shore grass, ghosts that would soon commence their eerie, chilly dance over the waters.

And Friedrich took a run-up to try and clear an obstacle. He knew he wouldn't succeed, he knew he'd get caught halfway, but he took his run-up, and he attempted it. He said: "This is just by chance, I've been given some money to do some work, I want to go traveling with the money, it would probably last me three months on my own, but it would be far, far nicer if you would come with me, and we could go through it together in a month or so. I think it would be wonderful to go with you to the edge of Europe, and look across at Africa. It's already hot down there, the oranges are ripe and plentiful on the boughs, you've never seen that, I've never seen it either, it's the landscape of the Greeks, those were the groves that Homer sang, come with me, what are you doing with yourself here in this cold and foggy and expensive city, what are you doing with yourself in this basement cabaret, with all those Russians, how did you ever get into that sweater club, come away with me." It was a good and a persuasive speech he had given, he had gotten impassioned, his optimism was aroused, as he ran up he almost believed he would clear the obstacle, he saw himself standing with Sibylle on some rocks, looking over the foaming waters of the Tyrrhenian Sea, and he saw to his delight that Sibylle was looking thoughtful and contemplative.

At last, she started fixing her salad, shook the bowl, mixed the whole thing up again, poured in oil and vinegar, shook salt and pepper over it, surely she must have ruined it, and then she said: "I can't. I've got a contract. I can't get away."

"Contract, forget it!" Friedrich made a sweeping movement with his arm, as though to set the world to rights. "Honestly, forget it. What kind of troupe is that? You ought to start acting again. Properly, in a proper theater. Do you remember how we used to rehearse you as Juliet, and how you used to make me cry, really howl, because you were so moving when you stood on top of the wobbly table in my room declaiming: 'Romeo is banished . . . Romeo is banished!'? You have to play her, play poor, cheated Juliet, properly on the stage, no one can ever have seen such a genuine Capulet princess. Come with me, and we'll practice the text, like Demosthenes on the beach, and everything will turn out wonderfully."

"No, no, I can't," she was putting up quite a fight, drumming her feet like someone being dragged away somewhere. "I can't. The troupe needs me. Anja needs me. Fedor needs me. Magnus too. And maybe Bosporus will come and see me. His leg is hurting him again. I have to be there for him. You see that, don't you?"

Yes, he could see that, there was nothing to be done. "But what's going on," he went on to say, "all of them depending on you, Anja, Fedor, Magnus, the whole troupe, what's that all about?" And once more he thought he was facing a storm, a block of sultriness under leaden skies, in which he would surely be asphyxiated, and from which he would be lucky to escape alive.

Sibylle did a little tiger pacing. The restaurant was empty. The waiters were dozing in the corners, it was a good place to stalk about, in among the rows of tables, in front of the lake's now-swirling fogs. She started to speak but broke off, just as she had done in her room in the morning. And once more Friedrich felt appalled: Had she turned cowardly, was she tangled up in some desperate intrigues that she was ashamed of, was she no longer master of the situation? "Oh, let it wait till tonight, you'll find out, wait till you meet Magnus and the others." She said the words very quietly. He made a move to stroke her hair, she let it happen a while, then she turned her head away and said: "Come on, let's walk by the lake for a while before I have to go to the theater."

They climbed down some steps from the terrace, and found themselves on a mole that led to the city's harbor. In summer, there was swimming here, ice-cream stalls and tents. But at this time, the mole, below the highway that led to Friedrich's hotel, was deserted. In the dingy light of dusk and lake fog, Friedrich and Sibylle were all alone, and felt cut off from the city and the world in general. They walked past heaps of bricks unloaded from barges, stacked in skewed red walls and small, squat piles. Cement crunched underfoot, scraps of coal, old buckets, household rubbish, ashes, dirt, and rubble. There were things flitting and darting out of cracks and holes. Maybe rats, they couldn't quite see. Why did Sibylle take this path? There was a chance that homeless people might be camping out here, beggars, evicted and desperate people who were condemned to lurk here like spiders till some victim ran into their arms. Sibylle thought of snow. She thought of white flakes, falling at a slant, and sharp cold. A damp miasma came out of the deeps of the lake. On the opposite side of the lake, the fog lamps were on again, flaky and milky, like fluffy dandelion heads. If the wind blew them out, I could play the Delphic game: loves me, loves me not, loves me, till I'm down to the very last flowerhead—but we're far past the oracle of scattered dandelion heads, Friedrich thought, shivering. He tried to put his arm round Sibylle again, as he had at lunchtime in the city. She started, and let it lie. Friedrich even thought he felt her body rest against his. Was she afraid? She had grown up in warm woolens and under the eye of a watchful mother, small and delicate: the Christ child, people had called her in her home by the river between the vine-clad hills. It had seemed horrible and unnatural, and humiliating in front of her friends, to be so cosseted and guarded. The cry "Mind you don't catch cold!" was to her a cry from hell. A curse that wrecked the day. She had suffered real, terrible childhood grief and never got over it, even today the tears came to her eyes when she looked back on it, the pain of not being allowed to go to school like other, rougher girls in her own class, in short socks in winter. The bare, cold legs of a classmate had been her desire and her torment. She had managed to capture the seat next to that girl in the classroom, and during class, Sibylle's hands never tired of touching the cool, bare skin of that other, envied girl under the desk. She would have liked to bite into that tempting flesh. It was her first love, and she didn't know it. A wintry passion: the joy of being a queen or a fairy-princess must certainly pale in comparison to this nonpareil of delight, of going about bare-legged in winter. Her mother turned a deaf ear to her pleas. So it was all Sibylle could do, occasionally, to tear the long, itchy, quite disgusting, woolen tights off her legs and secretly go barelegged in dark and empty lanes at night. Once, a stranger had seen and stopped her. She had shaken like a leaf, in her mortal dread. But when he had asked her: "Aren't you cold with your bare legs?" and stroked them with his hand, then she could have swooned with delight. And now she was leaning against Friedrich.

Even more mist had come off the lake and darkened the quay further. She lifted her skirts a little and let the wind blow against her knees and thighs. "I used to know boys," she said, "who still went swimming in October, and the time of the first snow." It was true, she really was pressing against him, pushing herself against his chest, like a cat, who wants to feel the petting hand still more. Friedrich held her. Held her in his arm. Held her fast, and wanted never to let her go. There seemed to be no one anywhere. It was doubtful whether a scream here would even be heard up on the main road. Her mouth against my mouth. Her lips parted, as though to drink. I have to kiss her now. Her breath in my face. The well is within reach. The source is flowing. I can drink, take a deep, liberating draft, feel the intoxication of the nectar of the gods, and never more awake into this world! He was a wolf at her throat. His eyes tried to gauge the distance to the water. He had even thought about dying with Sibylle. Once, high up on the topmost step of a high spiral staircase with a knee-high railing, he had thought: All I need to do is let myself fall, with my hands round her neck. And now again, the triumph grinned in him, to be, if nothing more, the last to drink from this mouth that had never been vouchsafed to him, and drain it. They stood barely two paces from the steep edge of the quay. They trembled together, like a tree in all its twigs. Her eyes were open wide, mirroring an infinity, as wide and deep and inapprehensible as a crack in a layer of clouds that suddenly opens up in front of a pilot, so that, dazzled by so much light, he suddenly succumbs in the dither of a fatal fall. They were swimming; her eyes, like flowing fire, were the eyes of a very young Sibylle, the eyes of a wild beast escaped from its lair, the irises were shining, and the pupils moved on the white sea between eyelids like two shining balls. Sibylle loitered in supernatural places. She was in a delirium of dream. Her hands clasped themselves round Friedrich's neck, and lay there as firmly as the chain on a door, and as tenderly as a rope woven from silk. His face inclined over her wind-contorted features in a steadily falling gazing; he thought someone was bound to come along at any moment, to push them calmly into death, and this time he did say, and the words broke the silence: "Little Sibylle"; and it roused her, and she came out of her spell, the twilight hour was over, and she said: "Come on, leave me be, and take your arm off of me, it's so heavy I feel it all down my back." And spontaneously, they both started running, wildly, dangerously, stumblingly, they ran madly and blindly, courting danger, as though it were a matter of catching up with life, and suddenly they were both afraid of collisions with the piles of bricks, of blows, of throttling hands and sharp rodent teeth. They were reeling when they reentered the light of the main road and the apparent security of civilization.

They made for the old town, through the crooked lanes that Friedrich had seen the night before as he was looking for the Diana Variety. It was seven o'clock. The little local grocers were shutting up shop. Fearfully they put up bars and grilles in front of the doors of their premises. Blinds came down with a jerk and a clank in front of the fly-spotted windows, and darkness swallowed the deathly pale detergent advertisements in their storefronts. It was the hour for taps and lights-out and evening roll call. The street, where at night only the big policeman had stood staring dreamily at his feet, was suddenly full of people. They rolled up, the musicians and the chanteuses, the bartenders and the waitresses in the bars bordering on the street. Great double-bass cases hovered like heavily laden balloons just above street level in the hands of short fat men. Drums, on the other hand, approached and passed like the wide gaping mouths of ships' cannons, pulled into position, in the raw red hands of long-armed young men with unpleasant coughs. A group of women stood in front of the main entrance to the Diana Variety. They were pressed back against the walls, to be out of the worst of the wind. In their featureless navy wool suits, and with their dull, submissive expressions, they might have been a bunch of housewives waiting for a department store sale to begin. Sibylle greeted them, and a few of them greeted her back, reluctant, measured, as though proud of occupying an inferior rank. Friedrich felt like calling out: *"Grüss Gott*, Mrs. Tax Inspector," but then he saw that these women were the girls whose almost naked photographs were on show in the glass vitrine.

"They're kept on a tight rein," Sibylle said. "They have to be here at seven sharp, but they never open the gates before quarter past. Magnus says he wants them to get some fresh air, because they don't get home till daybreak, and if it was up to them they wouldn't leave their beds."

"Does Magnus own the Variety, then?" Friedrich was astonished.

"Yes, he's the owner, but not the manager. He hates it really. He says he goes in there sometimes to make himself sick. But he lives off the takings. The whole city, he says, keeps it going. We live off their stupidity, he says to Anja, at dinner. Magnus's father was a wealthy man, a doctor and philanthropist, who left his entire fortune to a foundation for refugees. Magnus, his son, inherited three buildings. There's the St. Peter's Hostel, which he's not allowed to touch, this Variety Theater, and a little chalet outside the city, where he lives. Anja used to live there, she's married to him, but then she moved back into St. Peter's."

This was news. Friedrich thought: Why am I interested in this fellow?

They were standing a little back from the group of women, and Sibylle went on: "Magnus loathes these women. Cows, he calls them, cooks who can't cook, professional mourners who go onstage out of pique. Once, when he was still running the Variety, he tried to take on girls who, as he describes them, were like young, mulish, headstrong bulls; wild eighteen-year-olds, tanned, agile gymnasts, gazelles, chance offshoots of supple breezes, who, out of inborn dislike for any origins, were game for anything, even out of resentment against the boredom of their parental sofa world, *echt filles de joie*, hetaerae such as you find in the poems of Lucian. And the upshot of all his endeavors was that he practically went broke. The regulars stayed away, took their custom elsewhere, to the bars on either side. Only a few people with no money went, down-at-heel students with ragged trousers spent the whole night with eyes like saucers in front of a single glass of something that they were too preoccupied even to touch. The little guy who owns a dairy, a greengrocer's shop, or a pork butcher's, what he wants to see is his neighbor's wife, the woman he runs into on the staircase, the girl who's working for him, the housemaid who sweeps up the dirt in front of the steps down to his shop—figures from his day-to-day experience gyrating in front of his eyes in the tiny white glitter knickers of naked dancers, while he's hunched over a mug of beer or a glass of wine. That's the secret of the pleasure industry, a lesson that Magnus isn't able to apply personally, but [we live off stupidity] is happy to have applied by others on his behalf. He's a remarkable man, you'll get to see him in a moment, he's on his way; only leaving those poor girls out in the gale I think is a petty form of vengeance that isn't even worthy of a shriveled dwarf."

From the opposite side of the street, they heard a strident whistle. Fedor stepped into the light of a streetlamp and approached them. His walk was tired, and no longer as bouncy and insouciant as it had been that morning. He was carrying a small suitcase in one hand. A hotel stamp was stuck on one corner of it. Maybe it had his makeup things in it. It couldn't have been much. He looked like a salesman coming home after a trying day, without the least success. Over his sweater he was wearing a jacket. It was very tight and waisted. The stiff hat he had on in place of the cap that would have looked right with what he was wearing gave his appearance the element of posturing one might associate with a backstreet pimp. Only his face wasn't rosy enough. It's Russian, thought Friedrich, so incredibly Russian. It expresses the melancholy of those lugubrious tunes that are played by balalaika ensembles of ex-officers. Fedor shook hands with them both—kind, friendly, and unreserved. He gave off a slight whiff of alcohol, which suited his appearance to a tee. "What have you been up to?" he asked. "I've been running around all over the place." He was stateless, and was looking for a nationality that would supply him with a passport. Magnus, who by marrying Anja had made her a citizen of his country [which was probably the reason they had gotten married in the first place], had promised Fedor he'd adopt him. But now the authorities were making difficulties. It did not appear that Magnus had sufficient influence to get around them. Or maybe he wasn't serious about the adoption in the first place. That was Fedor's suspicion. He said: "There's something fishy going on." He was in a grim mood. "Come on, let's go down, it's cold. Did you and Friedrich have something to eat?" he asked Sibylle.

In the anteroom, the wardrobe women put on their starched white aprons. The beady-eyed cashier was already in place by the curtain that led into the auditorium. Her long fingers riffled the canary yellow tickets. She too seemed not to have stirred overnight. The notion that the whole world wanted nothing but to push past her into the theater poisoned her sleep and her time off. Fedor and Sibylle greeted her in passing. When they tried to take Friedrich through with them, however, she snapped shut. Fedor got agitated: "Friedrich isn't going to have to pay, is he?!"

"Either that, or he'll have to get a chit from Magnus."

So Magnus was her god, he was the one who counted, he was the one she obeyed. Friedrich hesitated; it was a disagreeable scene; he was perfectly willing to buy a ticket, but he thought it would demean him in front of the others. He said: "I'm just accompanying my friends to the changing room."

"Yes, but from there it's an easy matter to slip into the auditorium without paying."

"You seem pretty taken with the show!" Friedrich saw a way of ironizing the dispute: "I take my hat off to you." Coins chinked, there was a giving, a taking, and a changing.

Fedor said: "You're a fool, Magnus would have given you a chit."

Yes, of course, it was feeble of him, in spite of the pretense, but Friedrich didn't want to be seen to be scrounging a favor off

Magnus. In the auditorium, which was now fully occupied, the ranks of chairs were straight as soldiers on parade. "It looks pretty good," Friedrich said almost aloud. It was strange, the moment he ran into Fedor he felt like a bourgeois, a believer in cleanly swept floors, and order and decency and sobriety and moderation in all things. And this was Friedrich, who led a solitary existence cut off from any ties, and even as a child had favored all forms of gypsyishness.

They crossed the narrow stage, past wood blocks, nails, ropes, and pieces of cardboard, greeted a young fellow in blue overalls who was called Jupiter, probably because he tended the lights, and barged open the door to a room that smelled of laundry soap, combed-out hair, perfume, greasepaint, alcohol, dust, and rags. The changing room of the troupe. It was quite a large room, with curtained-off sections for men and women. The middle, the greater part of the room, was neutral. In any case, the curtains were still drawn, and Friedrich had to wonder whether they were ever made to do their supposed duty. In the middle of the room, facing the door, leaning over the window seat—a blacked-out rectangle that looked not unlike a photographer's studio background—stood the tall albino man, with eyes of runny aquarelle blue, that Friedrich had noticed the night before, resting his hands on the shoulders of Anja, who was standing in front of him, small by comparison, wrapped in her sheepskin, and puffing out smoke with an expression he couldn't see, as she had her back turned to the door. And it transpired that the giant was indeed Magnus, the son of that Doctor Magnus who had started the old foundation for "refugees of all nations."

An argument was in progress. Strife between Magnus and Anja.

The veins on the backs of his large hands were great, forceful canals. His will seemed to go straight into his hands; Anja's slumped shoulders trembled under their weight. His face, meanwhile, seemed calm, his mouth was closed, he didn't speak. And yet there was widespread disturbance, the others were talking and shouting. The room had filled up. The troupe was assembled. The boys in sweaters, the figure of the ancient peasant woman from bygone days, the sculpted Roman head of the lady in black tulle all spoke up, and Fedor also ran up, voicing his complaint. Shadows rose in Sibylle's face. Dissent was spreading, and her face was like a bright body of water, crossed by the great wingspan of a large night fowl, whose cawing, in popular legend, brings misfortune to the huts of those people who hear it. She returned to her makeup stool and her mirror. What possesses her to stay here, my God, why does she stay? thought Friedrich; that, and: If only I had a horse, a strong and mettlesome steed! I'd come galloping up and crash through the blacked-out windows, and snatch up Sibylle, and lay her across in front of me, and fly away, leaving in my wake only a shower of sparks from the impacts of the four stout, shod hooves of my mount. Oh, if only I had a horse! He almost said it aloud. Sibylle was fiddling about with boxes and bottles and pencils. A compact was knocked over, and a fine dusting of powder was scattered about the room like the white smoke of a locomotive as it whistles into the mouth of a tunnel, and left the arguing parties looking a little hazy, like people stepping out of East End pubs in London town on a foggy evening, the smoke of the wheat brandy in their throats, reeling in dazzlement, till they drown in the grimy, turbid milk that God, who also provided them with a blade to slit their fellow man's throat, spread over His streets. They were in danger, and so they showed their teeth. The ground they stood on was swaying. The immigration police had shown an interest in their enterprise, and they were to be deported. The members of the troupe were either, like Fedor, stateless, or else they had the passport of some nation that was not worth having. They enjoyed no diplomatic protection. They could not, when ordered to leave the country, puff out their chests and say: "Well, our embassy will have something to say about that, but for now we should put you on notice of the poor impression your decision will make internationally, and of the possible deterioration of the political situation that seems likely to follow from it." All this they could not do. All they could do was meekly bow their heads and appeal to the sympathy of some middle-ranking official. No country gave much for what happened to them. And as their situation was so bad, so desperate, so hopeless, so, correspondingly, their complaints were bitter, their cries of indignation frightful, and the tears in their eyes—tears of rage and shame and disappointment—genuine. Magnus had undertaken to plead their case in the name of his father's old foundation, appealing to the hallowed memory of his forebear, who had established the right to shelter and asylum. Had Magnus failed them? Did his connections not extend far enough? Was he not able to help, or did he not want to stand in the way of the departure of the troupe? Friedrich's view of things was as follows: He is the son, merely the son of the old Doctor Magnus who set up the foundation "for refugees of all nations," and it is with other sons that he will have to deal. There will be no chance for the troupe. The sons have never taken up the cause of the persecuted in a world where, any day, they themselves may be persecuted. For which of them, on getting up in the morning, can say with any certainty whether, amid the fates of the nations, in the turmoil of economics and the nightmares of rulers, of kings and ministers and managers of factories and mines—which of them is confident that his own death sentence has not, without a word to himself, been pronounced? The sons are unable to master life, and their consciences lie buried under the mountains of their fears. What do they care about someone from another nation, so long as they themselves are free from persecution, not forced to stand at others' doors and beg in others' languages? They turn away and ignore the needs of others, because need is a type of rejection, and carries the germ of death in it, so that no one dares to reach out a helping hand. And he felt sorry for Magnus. He is the son of old Doctor Magnus, who must have been an unusual man. And he is compelled to lug about the unusual inheritance, the unusual kindness and understanding perhaps, like a punishment with him. He has to look after the foundation, and talk to the ostracized. It's not that he lacks compassion. Don't condemn him! He is trying to hold on to Anja.

Friedrich started. Magnus was desperate to hold on to Anja. That was evident. The only reason he was still in the room was because Anja was standing in front of him, calling him names. He could have taken his hat and gone. It was on Anja's account that he was staying, ensuring by his being there that the earth didn't open under the troupe and send them plummeting to new depths. Was Magnus like Friedrich? Friedrich felt the similarity between their motives. He was here for Sibylle. Magnus was here for Anja. That struck Friedrich like a bolt of lightning. He didn't want to be like Magnus. He hated this mirror that was being held up in front of him. Only a moment ago, he had been ready to spring to Magnus's defense [he isn't heartless!] but now a wave of irrational anger crested in Friedrich. "Why won't you get these people residence permits? You are a citizen of this land. You owe it to the foundation. Why won't you furnish them with passports all round?" Friedrich's voice thrust at Magnus like a dangerously sharpened pair of scissors. The image of the lanky fellow with his watery blue eyes gave way in his imagination to that of a squat Cossack policeman, a gendarme in some Siberian place of exile; he saw ridiculous scenes, he saw Magnus, the son, sitting in his guardroom, with his saber buckled on, saw him dole out passports, imposing black documents with masses of red stamps on them. Had he, Friedrich, gone crazy? All the while, he wondered. His brain was functioning automatically, without any especial animus. All it was was just his desperation not on any account to resemble Magnus. Who stood there, like the victim of a lynch mob. A steppe had grown around him, and cut him off from the clean and well-governed city with its hefty constables pounding their beat. His hands had come in contact with the east in the form of Anja's shoulders, of little Anja with the soft mouth. Eyes he was unable to read branded his face. The steppes rose up against him. The fire flickered. Friedrich, impartial Friedrich, had given the signal. He was pushed forward, and set up against Magnus, eyeball to eyeball. It was the face of Sebastian the martyr that faced him. "You love Anja," he said, and his fury that there was another lover beside him in the world kept his voice trembling. "You love Anja, and that obliges you to look after every one of these people here. Can't you understand: Anja belongs first and foremost to her comrades, and only then, maybe, to you." Was he mad? Was he not thinking of Sibylle? He saw her outside the circle. She was putting on makeup, coarsening her face to look like that of a poor girl, driven to sing in courtyards. He was desperate to smash the reflection of himself that he could see in Magnus. Then he wanted to grab Sibylle and take her away with him, just as she was, smeared with paint.

Magnus let his hands fall from Anja, who had been standing woodenly in front of him, with a gesture as though he were letting her go. Tired, he murmured: "What do you know about the conditions and circumstances of our life? I do everything I can. I don't understand what possesses you, a stranger, to intervene in a quarrel you can't know the first thing about."

I really ought to take him by the hand, thought Friedrich, it is just exactly the way he's described it. But he's not a good man either. Friedrich pictured the line of scantily clad dancers waiting in the draft. The search for a good person oppressed him. How we all torment one another; must it be like that? He felt suddenly dizzy. He was uncertain, he moved back from his rebel leader's pose, and tried to burrow back into the ranks. A sensation of heat overpowered him. I can't believe it, I'm blushing. It was a feeling of shame he was unable to fight off.

He succeeded in forcing his way through the group, and back to Sibylle. "Get your bags packed. I'll come for you tomorrow morning at six at St. Peter's. You're coming away with me." Sibylle painted a horizontal black hunger line across her forehead. The line lay menacingly on her skin, like a dark thundercloud. "You can see, it's almost finished. Magnus can't do anything for you, what do you want to stay for? You'll end up being deported as well, and you haven't anything in common with these people who are real refugees. You've got a passport and a country and a consul behind you, you can turn your hand to something else; can't you see, it would be folly to stay on here."

Sibylle did not reply. She looked deeply into the glass, and checked her makeup. A layer of yellow on her lips gave her mouth a quality of decay. Then the excited huddle left the window, and Anja came up to Friedrich. A bell rang, Jupiter threw open the door and called in: "Come on, children, we've got a full house." And true, he could hear a hubbub of voices. The beady-eyed woman at the till had done good work today, she was disciplined, and seemingly untouched by the chaos she made possible.

Anja opened her mouth. She spoke loudly and clearly, everyone was meant to hear, no cigarette smoke blurred the sound of her words on this occasion: "I don't want Magnus thinking I'm going to stay with him if the others are deported. Every one of us will have to look for a place to go, we can't stay together, and I'm going to go with Friedrich. He's the only one of us I'd even consider." A resolute speech. A match flared at the end of it, and once again Anja drew the smoke of a cigarette in fervent gulps down into her lungs.

What was Friedrich to do? How should he respond? Was it possible to refuse? It had never occurred to him to take her with him. How could she put him in such a position? It made things terribly awkward with Magnus. He said: "But, but . . . " It was a mumbling and stammering. It didn't seem possible to offer an explanation that wouldn't offend Anja. Was she offering herself to him? What were her motives? Was she looking for protection, did she need help, or was he nothing but an escape route from her dependency on Magnus? He said: "I don't know if I have enough money for that. I only have a little, and I'm already taking Sibylle." His voice hadn't sounded as confident as Anja's. Fedor pushed away from Magnus and in the direction of Friedrich. Everyone looked at him. The young men had taken off their sweaters and were standing in front of their lockers in their little gymnasts' vests. The women were down to their underwear, or already half in costume.

Once again, the bell rang through the room. "First number, orchestra and beginners!" Jupiter, who had already turned up the stage lights, put his head through the door a second time.

Sibylle, all made up and in the tattered dress of the courtyard singer, leapt to her feet and knocked over her chair. "Are you mad? What gives you the right to make my decisions for me?" Her face was completely rigid. Under her makeup, her skin must be pale as marble.

"Sibylle!" He started trying to convince her.

Then Fedor was beside her, and his face once more was that of a man returning home from long and fruitless wanderings, sorry now that he will have to kill the dog who's whimpering expectantly to him. "You are a citizen," he said, turning to Friedrich. "Is that like a citizen? My God, don't you feel any sort of duty toward Anja?" His skin was gray, as though dobbed with flour, the black stubble sprouting through the sand. Wasn't it laughable?

Friedrich pressed his palms to his chest; then he brought them down, feeling the contours of his body. He wanted to make sure. Was it not possible that he was dreaming, that he was a man lying in bed asleep, watching himself with fear and trembling as the hero of a nightmare drama? Or was there some chemical transformation of the air, the fumes and vapors, the lack of oxygen he was breathing as in the inside of a gasometer that was befuddling his senses, and causing him to hear words that couldn't possibly have been said? The only certainty was that the scene was laughable, either way, and that he would have to draw strength to utter a scream to escape from the dream, and get out of this nightmarish tangle. "What about you," came the scream, "to whom 'citizen' is a dirty word, so that you curl your lip with disgust when you throw it at me? What allows you to live in bourgeois countries, under foreign laws that you despise, instead of going home to your country, which I seem to have heard is socialist, in accordance with the principles you profess? Why don't you go home and help build the new world that you call for in speech after speech? Is it that your revolution-ary strength is exhausted by wearing a symbolic sweater? You live in the revolutionary romanticism of the émigré who shuns any actual revolution because it would wreck his dim little world, the fairy-tale hour in poky restaurants with the hot soup of home that tastes so sadly familiar when sipped in exile?" Had he taken him on in a debate? Was he politicking? What was he doing, voicing these opinions? Emotion had told him what to say. Confusion, a rush of blood. Were his words sincere? He thought probably not. He went red, as after telling a lie he'd only later become aware of. Fedor's world was an empire of the dead. The shudders that went through Friedrich, they were genuine. He rejected that world. But didn't Sibylle live in it? Then he would free her. But was it possible to free someone who didn't want to be free? What were all those high-sounding words? Set free? Was that not the reason for his severity, the fact that he had been all ready and waiting to march into that world of Fedor's, to make common cause with the others, to be with Sibylle, and was it not just disappointment and dread not to have been called upon and not to have to leave, and was it not hate, the man-to-man hatred of Fedor, that prompted him to step forward with accusations [with accusations that were clean and sensible and for that reason were valueless if one wanted to be just], because Fedor was allowed to stay?

The faces of everyone in the room seemed to attack Friedrich. The unfinished masks of the comedians resembled the bloodthirsty expressions of fat ogres in Chinese stories. Fedor had a rebuttal all ready in his mouth, he was chewing it over before spitting it back at him, but Sibylle yelled "Shut up!" at him just as the mouthful was on the point of leaving his lips. She was like a drover. A radiant energy transformed her delicate, girlish appearance. She stood there, wide-legged and arms akimbo, like a young wrestler in a Roman arena, whose slender body in the course of murderous embraces has grown as sleekly muscular as a snake's. "And you go in the auditorium and watch, we're about to begin." She shoved Friedrich into the passage. Once again, he stumbled over the piles of rubbish behind the curtains. He entered the auditorium and stared into a hundred ranked, expectant faces. There wasn't an empty seat anywhere, and Friedrich sat down on a stool next to the piano at the foot of the stage.

The pianist struck some loud chords. His hands moved like those of a nervous man banging the tabletop in nervous desperation. He was a somewhat effeminate young man, and Friedrich was surprised at the brutality of his nimble fingers. The show was a success. There was laughter and cheering and sometimes people held their breath as an "aha" of discovery and agreement [silent, though;

this wasn't parliament] caused them to draw a deep breath. The satirical elements went down best. They went with the low, cellar-like rooms. Some scenes were put on in a garish poster style. Old moralities integrated into the construction of an asphalt city. The figure of the peasant woman from bygone days sang a setting of Villon. She stood there like a monument, massive and stone—Rodin would have been impressed—and she possessed the secret of all acting, which was presence: she passed over the stage like a cloud and she reached every member of the audience. She's gifted, by God she's gifted; the old ghosts come to life when they're stood in the limelight. Friedrich knew: then Sibylle would be lost. And he could only imagine what was going on behind the scenes, in the breaks between numbers, in the suspenseful moments of waiting to go on. It was the immemorial question about the leading lady's leading man. No man can bear it. He knows he will lose out. He would have to be an actor himself to lose his crazed fear that one day the actress, who by day holds actors in contempt, in the moment of her walking off stage, exhausted and disoriented in the real world, will sink into the arms of her partner, who had bided his moment to collapse backstage into a puddle of dust and sweat and greasepaint with the diva trembling with nervous exhaustion.

AND THAT was the hell into which he had delivered her. Friedrich remembered Sibylle's first public appearance. It was a drama school production. He had taken her to it. Better, he had dragged her there, like a calf to the slaughter. Of course, like everyone who had trained under the old director, she had to play *Lulu*, Act I, the scene in the Pierrot costume in the painter's atelier. She had been like a wild animal, beside herself with fear, excitement, and the vague pain of having to reveal herself. Early that morning, Friedrich had gone to collect her from the bed she had shared with Bosporus, still carrying the smell of him on her skin, and she was already ablaze. She had driven Friedrich out of bed for a "day of the naughty Sibylles." [On such days, they called each other the "S twins" and carried on like a variety act, swinging on trapezes in a winter garden.] On streetcars, they had been strangers calling each other names. In coaching inns, they discoursed in foreign tongues. On the escalator of the department store, Sibylle had contrived a fainting fit, and with wild gestures, Friedrich had dragged her backward downstairs, which had taken some doing, calling out: "My wife always suffers these attacks when she sees the rayon bosses in their frock coats." They had undertaken mysterious and highly suspicious measurement of civic buildings. They turned vague acquaintances into victims by walking up to tell them they had just been invited by telephone to attend a feast of shark fins newly flown in from Asia. Such days were wonderful, but they cost something too. They walked into cinemas, glanced at the screen, and said: "Dear me, how inappropriate, that woman's décolletage," and walked out again. They crisscrossed the city on open-top buses for the purposes of organized inverse theft. They had armed themselves with cheap children's watches and tried to stuff them undetected into other people's pockets. They thought how much more exciting it must be to find someone else's watch on you than to be missing your own. "Naughty Sibylle" days were days of happiness for Friedrich. Sibylle laughing, Sibylle merry, what did it matter that he tottered home exhausted, feverish, poor, hungry, penniless, and with no prospects? On the day of her first public appearance, however, it wasn't fun that drove Sibylle to these tricks but nerves. They had gone to Sibylle's apartment, and Sibylle had thrown herself on her—during the Bosporus period largely unused—bed. "Feel my heart," she had said. And her heart had lain under his hand. "Little Sibylle"—and even so he had delivered her. They had taken a taxi to the theater in the city center. Sibylle, who, for a laugh, was prepared to try the most risqué, exhibitionistic improvisations in front of partygoers, was now so shaky at the prospect of her debut that he had had to lie on top of her to calm her down. They had some brandy with them in a flask, and Sibylle drank it, and got drunk, without becoming any more valiant. On the way to the dressing room, she had lost her fear. She had puked while Friedrich held her trembling head. He had her hair in his mouth. She was a small creature, and devoted to him. He had left her in the passageway backstage.

Bosporus was in the auditorium. They sat together. Bosporus had no stains on his coat. That mattered to Friedrich, though it was unclear whether his emotion was pain or pride. Friedrich and Bosporus were friends. That was what Sibylle had wanted. Friedrich admired Bosporus, but there were times when he would gladly have murdered him. What does he know about Sibylle, it's a mistake [she isn't destined for him!]: that was what he had tended to think at such times. And then she had gone out onstage, after the shrill jingle of an alarm clock, and she hadn't been able to get a word out, she was drunk and distrait, but her movements had taken her through the scene, the movements of a gazelle leaping boldly over abysses. She allowed herself to be pursued, she knocked over props and fittings, the third wall fell over, the flame caught, the audience was uneasy, but Friedrich experienced a revelation of acting, a display of naked genius, a shy foal whose bolting gave promise of future triumphs, and Friedrich felt vindicated when at the end of the scene the director of the Kammerspiele had sent his card to Sibylle: "With my awe at your performance." Then they had gone out together, Bosporus and Sibylle and Friedrich. Friedrich had had to borrow money from Bosporus; and that hadn't been easy for him, but still easier than to leave the proximity of Sibylle and to decline the wine in which they were to toast her "dramatic career." They broke up outside Bosporus's apartment on the green canal bank. Sibylle and her lover [even so, she was not destined for him], he favoring his wounded leg ever so slightly, climbed up the stairs to bed. Friedrich had observed them through the glass of the front door. Was that a silent, wild peal of laughter that caused their shoulders to shake? Their heads, their shoulders, their backs, slid out of the top of the glass, and last of all their feet. With his hand on the heavy bundle containing the police revolver he had purchased from some criminals, his forehead against the glass, Friedrich had watched them go.

HE HAD stuck it out. He had loved her, and to the memory, they had been good days. He loved her still, and now that, once again, she was up onstage over him, was he to curse the boards she trod? She took her song to the people, her sad and tender little girl's song, and in the chorus the little girl was eaten up. Little Red Riding Hood is going through the forest. No Little Red Riding Hood sent by her mother with a bottle of wine for her grandmother, though. A little waif of a thing, and the trees formed up in two rows, it seemed they were actually office buildings, with paragraphs from the Constitution fluttering like flags on their roofs, and typewriter clatter coming out of their windows, and the wolf was driven up in an automobile, he was the Wolf of Wolf & Co., and he said: "Nothing under two thousand syllables, my honey," and he ran a thriving line in coffins in the basement. The movements were still hers, the gazelle leaps over the abysses, and everyone in the audience resolved to do some good deed on the way home, but by then they would have forgotten, so when the beggars stretched out their hands, no one would offer the homeless a bed for the night.

After Sibylle, it was the turn of Anja—the clown of the troupe, the prince's daughter—to be in the lights. Her sheepskin had stayed behind in the dressing room, and she had slipped into a sack. Properly crawled into it, and had the string drawn tight around her neck, under a cardboard mask, the stiff visage of a goblin, over her face. She took wobbly, shuffling steps. She was playing a sack of grain. The goblin-faced sack has eaten all the grain in the land. Now it feels sick and afraid. It's dizzy, it reels and falls to the ground. The tragedy of someone who's had enough to eat. Through the depersonalizing quality of the mask, it took effect. The audience howled with laughter. But was it really as funny as all that? Anja bowed. She took off the mask and held it in her hand. In the stage lights, she looked even paler and more coltish, and her mouth seemed even softer than by the ordinary light of day. It was Anja, who wanted to go away with Friedrich. A wave of tenderness, such as he had once felt for her already, came up in him again. But what about Magnus? Would Friedrich's prospects improve if he changed toward Magnus, whom he thought of as being in a situation resembling his own, and took the part of a seducer? If I take advantage of someone else's misfortune, then perhaps it will make me a different person.

A voice struck up and with a little effort filled the hall with song. Fedor leaned under a lamppost. On the edge of town somewhere. The lamppost and a bundle of old newspapers were meant to suggest the edge of town. The man under the lamppost stooped and picked up some of the newspapers. His singing was supposed to be what he read. The days passed, and truth went with them. It offered itself to anyone who came by, and it was always what they wanted to hear. That's Fedor, the balladeer of simple truths, he has barely enough strength to sing. Friedrich felt fresh antipathy toward him. I haven't washed all day, he thought, and he looked with displeasure at his hands, which were streaked with dirt. He had no more interest in the cabaret. The somnambulism of art, which had held him for a while in the guise of the peasant woman from a bygone age, and Sibylle's song, and Anja's dance, was now less than enthralling. Friedrich longed for fresh air.

The street looked much as it had the night before, when he had first stood and gazed at the girls' pictures in the vitrine. Friedrich was practically the only person around. He pulled his coat tight and walked up and down outside the theater, like a policeman on his beat. The light of the DIANA VARIETY THEATER sign spilled over him. He was sorry he didn't smoke. A cigarette would have been a good prop. He wanted to come to a decision. It had been a mistake to go down the stairs to the basement theater. Everything had been a mistake. He had slipped out of his role. The role of the gentleman passing through, polite but basically uninterested. He clenched his fists and stamped on the ground. I must leave immediately, I'm not up to this, I don't have the stomach for it, if I stay for the end of the show, I'll go crawling into the dressing room like a dog, licking the dirt off their shoes, a repulsive whining creature, begging to be allowed to stay and sniff their skirts. His legs took him away. He left the spot, ran off. That was it: He saw himself walking on the edge of a half-frozen lake, in the middle of which Sibylle was skating, and he ran away into the forest, so as not to have to save her at the moment she crashed through the ice.

He actually had broken into a run. But was his scene not a piece of devilish deception? Had it not always been the other way around, that he had rescued Sibylle and had himself drowned every time, and died, so that he was no longer entitled to be a rescuer? He ran past the policeman staring down at his feet, who raised his white stick: "What's the hurry?"

"Thirst," panted Friedrich.

His feet dragged him up the four stone flags. Then it was as though he had been stood in the smoke of a chimney breast. Human shadows slunk around him. He grabbed hold of the bar— a brass life belt. "Brandy and soda." He was given a glass and swallowed the contents like a bitter medicine. He felt alive once more. A notion came to him. He saw a fat girl smiling at him from behind the bar. "Where am I?" he asked. "I mean, what's the name of this pub, what's the address?"

The girl took his words for a come-on. She said: "I'm sure you know perfectly well where you are," and laughed as though it was the funniest thing.

Friedrich hit the brass rail with his fist: "Come on, quick, I want to know!" The girl was sluggish, what was the stranger playing at? She cheerfully told him the name of the bar, the street, and the number. Friedrich wrote it all down. Then: "I'd like to place a telephone call."

The telephone hung on the back wall. Friedrich was obliged to stand between two couples, who broke off their embraces and stared at him with hostility. It seemed to take an eternity before the operator came on. He asked to speak to the Diana Variety Theater, the downstairs cabaret.

"I need a number from you," the stern voice told him.

"I can't, I don't know it, please don't hang up on me." Friedrich pleaded and urged: "It's the Diana Variety Theater, it must be an easy matter for you to find it."

The voice remained pedantic and unyielding: "I'll pass you on to information," it said.

Another eternity passed. Had the telephone been invented as an instrument for the torment of lovers? Information came on, fresh explanations, fresh objections, at last he was furnished with the number, then back to the stern voice, a further eternity, then a clicking in his earpiece, a fresh eternity, finally a sonorous bass voice, the bartender of the cabaret, thank God it was the bartender rather than a member of the troupe. Friedrich said Sibylle's name. "Listen please, it's important, she has to come to the phone, quickly, it's urgent." A thousand eternities, a thousand sounds in the earpiece pressed to his straining ear, desperate, terrified, while his unoccupied right hand flapped nervously, to try to calm the noise all around.

Sibylle came on, sounding thoughtful and hesitant. "Oh, it's you," she said. "Where have you got to?"

Friedrich flew at her. He would have bitten through the telephone. He wanted to seize her, and carry her off. "Sibylle," he screamed, "I'm waiting here, you've got to come away with me, you've got to, you can't stay there, I'm waiting for you, I'm expecting you, we're leaving tonight." He described the landscapes that lay ahead of them, he heightened, he exaggerated, he launched himself into the comfort of the hotels, which were such that he couldn't possibly have afforded them, he assailed her with a torrential waterfall to rob her of her senses.

She said: "Just wait a minute, don't go." And once more there was an eternity to wait. He harkened like a man digging his ear into the ground to listen to the breathing of the mystery of life within it. He heard footsteps that drew reluctantly nearer, then her voice was there, sounding teary [as Friedrich would tell himself later] and uncertain and gently caressing: "Friedrich, there's a night train. In one hour. Be at the station. Buy a second ticket, take a couchette in the wagon-lit. And . . . " Maybe there were more words on their way to him, but they were no longer audible. A rushing sound, like a tap, filled his listening ear. Maybe Sibylle had broken the connection.

HE LISTENED to the shifting and creaking in the bed overhead. Then perfect silence was restored to the compartment. Only the glimmer of a cigarette still left its hot reflection on the white paneled ceiling of the carriage. Each time light fell into the space, for seconds at a time, light from the stations, light from snowy fields, starlight, there were girl-things to be seen on the floor of the compartment, lying there in a disorderly scatter, mouse-gray stockings, a soft ivory colored chemise with a yellow animal's head stitched over the heart and a lace edge on the triangle of a pair of tumbler's panties. *I'm traveling with a girl, I'm going across the Alps. I'm traveling with a girl, I'm going across the Alps*. The sentence tumbled along with the wheels. It fitted the rhythm of their revolutions perfectly. A clear and simple thought, one could say it over and over again to oneself: "I'm traveling with a girl, I'm going across the Alps." It would sound good drunk.

Friedrich had wrapped up his stay in the city quickly and decisively. From the place where he had made his telephone call, he had traveled straight to the hotel by the lake, and had called out to the fellow in the hall, the black god in his tailcoat, standing in front of his ranks of scarlet-and-white-satin page boys, that he wanted to settle his bill, and immediately [this last with the raised voice of a company director], he was leaving, yes absolutely right away, on the night express in an hour. Then, a victor, a conqueror, a triumphant hero, crowned darling of the gods, he had hastened to his pauper's cell in the abode of the rich, had laughed at the bars outside the window, thrown together his belongings, and tossed the telephone directory up at the ceiling. Let the names fall where they might, what did he care about other people's names? They could be dentists or engineers for all he cared, let them live and die in the foreign city, it was nothing to him, he was leaving, happiness had come for him, he was living once more, and leaving with Sibylle, he imagined himself a second time standing with her in the light of the Hellenic sun on some goatherd's rock, ringed by southern seas. One of the pages had come for his suitcase, and in his exuberance Friedrich scorned both stairs and elevator, and slid down the balustrade feet out and arms wide so rapidly that he couldn't control his descent and came to a stop at the feet of the suddenly frozen black god.

At the station, he bought tickets, he took a compartment with two bunks, just as Sibylle's voice had said on the telephone. And then the waiting began. No Sibylle. But she would come; she had to come; she had said she would. But where would he find her? The station was enormous. Maybe she was already there, as he was, waiting and panicking. The station seemed to grow. It stretched out and spread and went off into the distance. There was one hall after another. Friedrich saw himself as an ant in a termite burrow. His fear of missing her made him feel sick. In the end he rushed out into the departure hall. The platforms were not blocked off. He asked for his train. A clock showed its shining face. The big hand moved ever closer to the minute of departure. It was a decidedly unpleasant clock, as evil as the time clock at the entrance to the lightbulb factory. The hand bit into time like a tooth. It ate the minutes with an avid crunch. Travelers ran past Friedrich, followed by panting porters. He was bumped by suitcases, and he lost himself in the daydreams that took him. He saw himself as a foreign traveler with urgent business. Also he saw himself as one of the panting porters: the man weighed down and the man obliged always to remain behind. How lucky I am, he thought to himself, to be leaving with Sibylle. The increasingly frantic cries of newspaper vendors, fruit sellers, and cigar sellers, the increasingly monitory calls of the conductors, and the squeals of brakes being tested, all sent waves of sweat down his back. He raced down the length of the train. "Sibylle! Sibylle!" He was shouting. People turned to stare at him. Then in front of the blue sleeping car Anja appeared, the daughter of the prince, little Anja in her shaggy sheepskin, a cigarette in her soft mouth, a round, cracked leather case next to her [it even had a scraped sticker from the GRAND HOTEL ROMANOV, PETROGRAD], holding a letter in her hand and casually leaning back against the side of the carriage.

"What is it, what's going on, where's Sibylle, is she inside already?" Friedrich blurted, the words falling over each other.

Anja's expression was utterly calm. She held out her hand with the letter in it. It was addressed in Sibylle's large, clear, roman, and perfectly even childish hand. "She's not coming!"

Friedrich slumped against the side of the carriage. He tugged at the envelope, and it took a while before he held the page of a letter in his trembling hand. "HEE-HEE-HEE, HO-HO-HU, HA-HA-HA" ran the first paragraph in large letters drawn across the breadth of the page. There followed three rapidly scrawled lines, as if Sibylle had been running away from them. "Live only by your wits," he read, an allusion to a song. "Your wits won't feed more than a louse.[2] I must stay with Fedor, and Anja has to leave Magnus for a while. Have a nice trip: your Sibylle." There followed one more

[2] "The Beggars' March" from *The Threepenny Opera* (1928) by Brecht and Weill. The Willett/Manheim translation reads:

> Mankind lives by its head
> Its head won't see it through
> Inspect your own. What lives off that?
> At most a louse or two.

paragraph at the bottom of the sheet, clearly written this time, and added perhaps to console him: "If you haven't guessed by now: I'm the old woman who lives next door, though you don't know what I'm for—that's the song we sing in the dressing room, and you may sing it in blithe and cheerful fashion, by special permission of Sibyllchen and the Management." Hammers dropped from the sooty glass bell of the hall. Friedrich was sightless; neither Anja nor the train existed for him. "All aboard, ladies and gentlemen, all aboard," called the conductors. Doors slammed shut. Hands pushed him helpfully up the steps. His suitcases were slid in after him. Another door banged shut, the mouse was in the trap, the train began to move. In the light of the platform, waving arms were left behind.

Friedrich was still clutching the letter. Without discerning any outlines, his eyes rested on the lit-up rooms in the houses next to the tracks. Then the letter was gone. He must have put it down somewhere. It didn't matter anyway. "Your reservations, please," said the conductor. "May I see your reservations, please? Monsieur and Madame have beds fourteen and fifteen, thank you." So we're monsieur and madame now, thought Friedrich. How funny, he thought, with a serious attempt at laughter. And also: I wonder whether the conductor would continue to say "monsieur and madame" if I were to pull off my shoes and run down the corridor like a gorilla, smashing all the windows as I went. But he lacked the strength even to untie his laces. "May I have your tickets as well, please," the conductor went on, "so that Monsieur and Madame won't be disturbed in the night." How nice, we won't be disturbed! The conductor took the tickets. He received a tip as well; naturally, his care deserved a tip, everything smoothly took its course, as befitted a monsieur and a madame.

They were on their own. The door had been closed on them. As yet, not a word had passed between them. Here, in the narrow space at the foot of the two bunk beds, there was no escaping the other. They stood and faced each other. What does she think will happen? Friedrich wondered. Is she expecting me to slap her across the face? That I take hold of her and throw her out of the window? Anja looked at him. Her face was unchanged in its utter tranquillity. Her look seemed to go past Friedrich and out into infinite space. This is the end, thought Friedrich, the living end. He raised his two hands toward Anja, and they fluttered up and settled on her shoulders like two birds. Like Magnus, as he was trying to appease her! They stood so a while, both of them very serious. Is Sibylle sleeping with Fedor? He didn't even think she was; it didn't seem enough for Sibylle; he wanted to bewail the loss of a queen. He took Anja's head in his hands and kissed her on the mouth. He did so thinking she needs to be told that I won't throw her out. Her lips tasted of tobacco, and they were cool and dry like the lips of a child. "Top or bottom?" he asked, gesturing at the bunk beds.

"Top," she said. Thereupon he laid himself, just exactly as he was, on the lower bed, while she took off her dress. She had the attractive curves of a girl, and a firm bosom. Friedrich had expected her to be a little more boyish. "Good night," she said, and she clambered into the top bed.

"Good night," said Friedrich. He got up once more, to open the window and switch off the light; then, dressed as he was, he rolled himself up in the sheets.

It is sometimes good to travel like a banker, or a fraudster. Bedded on soft mattresses, even worried souls get to where they want to go. Whereas those who endure the hard planks of third-class accommodation will never reach the kind station of their destination. Adversity forces one to recognize the futility of human endeavor, it makes for insight and compliance. Wakeful nights scrape the deceit of optimism from one's expression. With naked and battered visage, the traveler steps into the corridor in the morning and is assailed by the pale and nimble specter of the new day, chasing the train across the meadows, leaping in at the window, and pressing the exhausted traveler as he struggles for breath, till he is prepared to confess and to implicate himself. But Friedrich, by taking the night train over the mountains [like a banker, or again a fraudster], experienced a magnificent riot of the senses. He rested, the while the blue carriage climbed ever higher. He could follow the process. Like fast-forward movements in a fantastic film, the night charged by into Friedrich's view, as he gazed out of the interior of the darkened compartment toward the rectangle of the open window. He experienced the surge and sway of the ride, the steep corners, the furtive shadows and leaping lights, the flats of snow, walls of ice, crystal waters, violet-colored gulfs of fog, holes in the deep sky, cloud gallops, stars, red and green signals, white lamplight over the deserted platforms of remote mountain stations, shining slate walls of tunnels, endless winds, storm currents in the air, pure and powerful aromas, dust of snow, as occasional swirls in the rise and fall of the journey. It was a journey like a drug rush, and it most resembled the reeling experienced by sensitive listeners as they concentrated on certain musical sequences.

And yet those notes, coming to him from outside, were only the accompaniment and the amplification of the melody that was in his heart.

The weak reflection of a cigarette glow under the ceiling of the compartment was gone. Was Anja already asleep? Friedrich listened. He couldn't hear her breathing. What about Sibylle? He didn't need to fight the idea that she could be sleeping with Fedor. That idea was completely absurd. It wasn't even that Fedor was too lowly; Sibylle had had fleeting relationships with still lowlier types, in Friedrich's view, and Sibylle had even admitted the inferiority of these passing fancies of hers. "It's just what I felt like," she had said. But Fedor struck Friedrich as just not worthy. It can't be any fun to have a poor man come home to you. Friedrich could only imagine Fedor in the exhausted posture of a little man without any deeper insight into things, and then, once home, or in a circle of others like himself, raging against this world in order to refuse all blame or responsibility for it. Sibylle couldn't love Fedor. That much seemed clear. Friedrich accounted for their chumminess, as he tried to term it to himself, with reference to Sibylle's loyalty to the capital of her country, where Fedor had performed and known people and was able to name places and streets and events. He'll just be there to give her memories a cue. And so Fedor played no part in the deception that had just been practiced on Friedrich. Friedrich didn't hate Fedor. He merely envied him, as he envied anyone who was allowed to live in Sibylle's proximity. Other than that, he didn't care one way or the other about Fedor. The deception was purely Sibylle's. At the most, Anja might be a peripheral figure in the plan. Anja had wanted to get away from Magnus, and Sibylle loved playing the role of a knight in shining armor to young girls. Why shouldn't she help Anja to get away on a trip? Maybe the whole thing was just a joke. It struck him as possible that Sibylle had thought to herself: What if I send along a substitute? She was certainly capable of it. Perhaps it was foolish of Friedrich not to avail himself of the substitute. Maybe a girl was just a girl, and all his woe and agitation could be settled biologically. He listened again for sounds of sleep or vigil over his head, but there was nothing. Friedrich felt his heart. Once again, it was the frightened bird palpitating in a stranger's large hand. He thought: If Anja were to sleep with me, I wouldn't do anything to hurt her, but she could give me the sense of another body next to mine, she could warm me and take my heart away from the stranger, and put it back in my breast. He knew his idea of their chastely lying together was a sentimental one, but that didn't bother him just then. In certain shocking predicaments, in spite of the unsentimental century, a man yearns for a creature he can stroke. And while cats and dogs and other animals are not routinely lent out to the sorry, wakeful occupants of international sleeping cars for the duration of their journey, he at least had Anja there with him. Even so, he was reluctant to wake her. Only when light happened to fall on the girl-things on the floor, light from stations, light from snow plains, starlight, he thought for a moment of calling to her; but even as he was thinking about it, the idea disappeared among others in his head. What if Sibylle had come? What if they were her things instead of Anja's that were lying on the floor? If it was the sound of her breathing he was trying to hear? How would it be with him then? Not the deceitful fantasizing (*I'm traveling with Sibylle*), but suppose she had actually come and it was Sibylle asleep in the top bunk? Did he not have it in him to think in more generous ways, and so wasn't it a matter of indifference whether Sibylle was sharing the same wagon-lit, or the same planet? What further benefits could accrue to him from her nearness? A greater degree of excitement. But couldn't he derive that from her distance too? Did the thoughts he was having on this nocturnal journey mean that his love for Sibylle was over? By understanding this love as an arduous task that he had put behind him, he might be able to keep it going by compiling a catalog of his torments, raking them together from the field of past time where they sprouted, into a bonfire over the pain of his latest disappointment.

He was benumbed. He kept wanting to utter her name. But never in the course of that night did it take the form of a crazed brutal yell over the thunder of the train, the rattle of the wheels, the whistle of the locomotive, the echo of the valleys. Was it that the heart of the "monsieur" in the sleeping car was already too old to love and rave and burn? Back when, following the night in the lamp room, the electric shock from the storm of little lightnings in the suddenly extinguished inferno, and the morning contretemps with Beck, when he had gone round to Sibylle's in the afternoon to pick up his keys—back then he hadn't been a "monsieur" yet, traveling across the mountains at night in a compartment with a girl he barely knew.

WHEN BECK left the room, Friedrich had leapt up out of bed. I need to get hold of some money, he thought. He had still felt a little wobbly on his legs and woozy in his head, floppy just about everywhere, particularly his heartbeat, but the measure he proposed to take could be done in his sort of sleepwalking condition. He bundled up everything he had by way of old and worn clothing, he could no longer go around dressed like that anyway, and went to the street by the wall to offer them for sale to the secondhand clothes dealers who lived there. The secondhand clothes dealers looked at what Friedrich spread out on their tables, as if they were loathsome toads that you had to keep away from your body with fire tongs. Friedrich, desperate for money, was too inexperienced to understand that the secondhand clothes dealers were behaving just as they always did, and wanted in fact to buy what he offered them. When, at the end of a contemptuous spiel, they offered him a few pennies—purely out of pity for him, "so you haven't had a wasted journey"—he was so astonished that he thanked them. It wasn't until he was back on the street that it dawned on him that he was still poor after this transaction. But he believed that everything depended on money. He wanted to appear before Sibylle like a prince from Arabia, offering wondrous presents and having the magical ability to fulfill all desires instantly and with a smile, as though he had Aladdin's lamp, at the very least. On none of the hungry days he had lived through had the thought of being poor struck him so forcibly, like a curse, like a dismissal from the sight of God and from the joys of His worldly table. An aphorism of La Bruyère's struck him: "It is a calamity to be in love and not to have a large fortune!" He would have been willing to scrabble in the dirt to reach the means of granting wishes and of supporting love. He hastened to exploit whatever possibilities he had. Where only recently modesty and breeding would have prevented him from applying, he now saw possibilities. He thought it must sometimes happen that bank messengers drop their envelopes, so he focused his eyes on the muck in the gutters. He cursed a world in which one could no longer sell oneself to the Devil [but later, he was of the view that he had indeed made a contract with the Devil, but on less favorable terms]. And after that he went scrounging. He was completely unscrupulous in this, and possessed a naive aptitude. His motto was that the end justified the means. He called on a few people, telling them about his recent accident at night and of the need for an expensive treatment. What he managed to raise in the course of these depredations had by lunchtime come to almost fifty marks. His victims said of his visits that they had felt obliged to help him out because they had never seen anyone with an expression of such desperate need. And with fifty marks Friedrich felt rich. He went to a barbershop to have his untrimmed beard taken off, and he had his hair washed with fragrant shampoos and cut, and his face invigorated by the application of hot towels. And he went out to lunch in an expensive restaurant. He didn't say so to himself, but what drove him was the desire to appear at the top of his form when he next saw Sibylle. And he drank a glass of Burgundy, to settle his heart and nerves. Then he bought some large yellow chrysanthemums and went round to Sibylle's apartment on the square in front of the KDW department store.

Even as he was going up the stairs, he was saying to himself: "Maybe I'll be able to do something to help Beck." He said it and stopped, because of the thought, tall and bright like a celestial star: She is predestined for me! He rang, and the room he was ushered into was immense. But it wasn't the starlet's apartment of which he had spoken mockingly to Beck, following Beck's description of it. It was an immense room in which the resident had so spread herself that she conquered it, whereas most tenants are in thrall to their rooms. The first thing Friedrich noticed were the books. They lay around all over the place, on tables, chairs, suitcases, cushions, and the floor. Next he saw animals. Brown teddy bears, gray woolly donkeys, white fluffy goats, wheeled elephants with magnificent red and gold harnesses. Picture books. Watercolors. A ticking railway set. Clothes. Materials. Ribbons and scarves. And bottles and flagons with powder, makeup, and tinted waters. Chinese dolls. A theater in which Death and the Devil were embracing. And many, many balls. And there, on a little rug in the middle of the room, in front of an electric reflector fire, lay Sibylle. She had barely anything on. Only a white silk shirt that permitted the heat to shine on her skin, and holding in the shirttails a little pair of swimming briefs, the triangle of a champion swimmer. As she jumped up to say hello, he sank to his knees on the floor. He was putting on a rather theatrical version of a greeting, to conceal his awkwardness. He still had the chrysanthemums in his hand. He saw she had legs like two slender columns, shining and firm and ivory. She's so perfectly made, she's like the young of some animal. God must be proud of her, thought Friedrich as he fell to his knees.

Then, on the other side of the equator, as Sibylle called the strip of the room that was nearest the heater, someone moved, a man. He moved away from the desk he'd been hunched over, with his back to the door, and turned to face Friedrich. His face showed he'd been hard at work. Friedrich stood rather stunned by the ravages of the concentration that flickered in little flames around the man's eyes. He couldn't be any older than forty, but his slumped posture, his gray jowls and thinning hair, all spoke of a man used beyond his years. "That's Walter," said Sibylle. Friedrich wanted to shake hands with the famous critic, but the man made no move toward him. He didn't budge from his desk, and betrayed the signs of a tension that seemed to have seized him like a cramp. He's not a happy man, thought a shocked Friedrich. He's famous, respected, and admired; he is a power in his particular field, the theater people and the playwrights all tremble when they know he's writing something about them; he makes enough money for food and clothes and to keep this splendid room with all its books and animals; and he is allowed to be with Sibylle, he takes her to restaurants and theaters, he lives with her, though she isn't predestined for him, and he isn't happy.

Friedrich was disappointed by Walter, and furious at him. Without having thought about it before, he had expected the man to leap out and fling his arms around everyone and exclaim: "Look at her, isn't she lovely!" And then Walter did call out her name: "Sibylle!" and it was a cry, and Friedrich understood that this man loved her, and he saw in him torments that he knew were soon to be his as well. Walter had, as they said in the circles in which they moved, "had" Sibylle, and he remained someone she respected, but since he loved her, and didn't merely want to "have" Sibylle but to keep her for himself, he was bound to quit the field having lost her. The cry "Sibylle" didn't deserve her retort: "If you're feeling like that, why don't you go?" Friedrich blushed to witness such a parting. It affected him in spite of himself that a man would risk one cry, then nothing more, and walk away from his room and his work.

Sibylle explained. She said: "He's not the type to vault over the table at you. It takes him time. He's ambitious and slaves away like a student before final exams. It's unbearable. He insists he can only give of his best here in my room. I need to be there for it to happen. He always wants to be near me. First I had to sit in front of him in the window, and now in winter I'm at least allowed to lie behind him on the equator. It's sooo boring. I invite people round to see me, and that makes him so furious he can't write another line. So he has to go out and drink, even though it means he gets trouble from the newspaper later." No one had accused her of anything, but she justified herself: "He's so jealous, I simply have to deceive him. It's nothing to me, but when he takes me home at night and then stands by the door and looks at me like a dog and begs me to go to my little beddie-byes and stay there, he's really forcing me to sneak back down the stairs in the dark a few minutes later, and go off somewhere. And afterward word gets out. Of course, I'm not trying to do anything behind his back. Once as I was leaving the house, I saw him lurking behind the kiosk. He followed me. I was aware of him. I could have driven off in a taxi, or turned round and gone back inside and just pretended I'd wanted to take a little walk. Maybe I really didn't want to do anything more. But his shadow trailing after me forced me to go to this man who had asked me to see him. He's as possessive as a cannibal of a white virgin."

"Then will he hate me too?" asked Friedrich.

"Sure. He sees me falling into bed with everyone. His friend Franz once said ideally he would carry me in his wallet."

Walter the critic's love for Sibylle on that day was still a way for Friedrich to reach her. All he needed to do was conjure up for her the picture of Walter in the lowest pub in the area still tasting the touch of her lips, which, in Walter's aroused condition was steady and obscene. Sibylle could have acted in accordance with Walter's mistaken notions. She always did as she pleased, with the single exception that she never did the worst thing that was expected of her. That law could be made to work in his favor. But Friedrich was still shocked by the expression and the cry of the great man, and was unable to do anything to hurt him. All he wanted was to put his case, and Beck's case, next to Walter's. Then Sibylle could decide between them. He thought himself wise and just, and he was the victim of youthful, romantic mistakes. He didn't understand that he was dealing falsely by his rivals [he thought it was wise; in fact, it was stupid] by putting his trust in the strength of his love (*she is destined for me*) and was full of hope that he might win her by these methods he called fair. Sure, Walter loved Sibylle, but his love was certainly not as all-embracing as Friedrich's, because how, Friedrich went on to think, could Walter confine his jealousy to other men, while Friedrich was already envious of the air in the room for being allowed to touch Sibylle?

Evening had arrived in all its pomp. An advertisement danced up and down the front of the department store, and a fiery red glow jumped sporadically into Sibylle's room. They were lying on the equator. Friedrich too had lain down. He held her left hand in his right. Though slender and delicate, it felt firm. He said: "I love you, Sibylle," and he supposed the passion that prompted him to say the words must cross over from his heart, through their hands, and reach hers. Later on, he would mock himself with a bitter taste in his blood: Just then, I must have been a good person, an open char-

acter, and that made me defenseless, naked and open to ridicule.
He deemed it necessary to talk about himself, to present himself,
to unmask himself. He told her about a boy he had been in love
with at school, he talked about the Swedish girl student with her
blond hair under a white cap that was like a breaking wave in the
summer sea outside the town, he talked about sensitivity, about
how he'd fallen in love with a gesture, a walk, a scent, a laugh, he
admitted the temptations of sore dreams in the hour of falling
asleep, and reported to her of the joy of a readiness to be in love,
though always under the control of his will. He didn't dissemble or
improve anything. He described his early years, the sacrifices he'd
made and the pleasures foregone, an asceticism that was voluntary
because he was too proud to take part in the pleasures of the clod-
dish young people at the university, and too poor to pursue the
slender dancers that he'd worshiped from afar in the theater, from
up in the gods. And he talked about work he had undertaken, of
difficulties that stood in the way of his getting a good job, and end-
lessly of his hopes and desires and future dreams, and that the sum
of this picture and of his days now no longer mattered, and had
been invalidated, thrown over, broken, redirected, by his understanding that he loved Sibylle, by the certainty of his feeling that he
had to love her, her of all women, and only her. The portrait that
had been placed in front of Sibylle wasn't that of a standard contemporary young man. Nor was it like the youth of any young man
of Sibylle's wide acquaintance. She felt the urgency that was
expressed in the claim: You were meant for me. Never at any time
in the future would she claim not to have understood the passion
that had filled Friedrich, and to which he had subordinated his

whole self and being. She felt addressed. It was she who raised her hand, and pulled him down toward her, but it was she as well who firmly and decisively pushed away the head as it flew down toward her, and let him fall, in her fear that she might be lost to herself. There are some who say she wasn't yet ready for love, she hadn't yet slept around sufficiently, but it is Friedrich's belief that at the moment he was to receive the woman who was destined for him, his own devil got control of the girl's soul and endowed it with ever more magnificent attractions, with understanding and cleverness, with fun and kindness and courage and all the qualities that lead us to love, lead us to love wholly and profoundly, to give ourselves without holding back anything, not only to the body of the other— the pretty larva that fades, that passes, the breasts whose roses wither, the soft skin that under the bloom of sweet seventeen already bears in itself the gray pigmentation of age, the arms and legs and torso, whose firm flesh one day will be flabby or blood-lessly scrawny—fallen not just for the appearance but much more for the beloved's soul, a need to loiter in her breath and her blood-stream, to be a child in her womb.

"Be a good fellow and call Beck. I like it when it's the three of us, together. I want to go out and eat." Sibylle had leapt to her feet. She reached for a coat, and draped it over her shoulders. The "be a good fellow" was somehow ladylike. She said it in a tone of: "I'm not really like that, but it's the way I talk to you." Were they playing "puss in the corner"? No, the war had broken out, and it wasn't just a little girl's revenge: Yesterday it was your turn to be stiff and aloof, today it's mine. The war had broken out and he had lost. Friedrich called Beck. They agreed to meet in the wine bar. He no longer had the willpower to go away and leave Sibylle alone with Beck. And that wasn't what Sibylle wanted to happen either. She didn't want to be with Beck any more than she wanted to be with Friedrich. And consequently, she found them an agreeable team together. And Beck came up trumps. In those days, he pulled his weight valorously. Friedrich and Beck didn't want to be themselves. That was embarrassing to each of them. And so they metamorphosed, addressed one another by outlandish names, held conversations in languages they didn't know. Russian was especially good to mimic. They attained such mastery, even when they were by themselves walking down the street or in a bar, that they could speak in their imaginary language and understand one another. Sibylle was as happy as a little girl at a funfair. "I've wet my undies," she screamed, and let them feel for themselves, because when she was laughing she couldn't remain decent, she was so happy and she really was a child, and neither Beck nor Friedrich found anything odd or obscene about her. They played drunk. They drank water from little vodka glasses and shuddered after each swallow. "Ha, ha, ha," they went, reeling, clutched at the tablecloth and pulled the whole thing down on top of them. "God, that was great!" Sibylle hadn't had so much fun in ages. They took a taxi and shouted abuse at the pedestrians. Sibylle stuck her legs out the window: "People need a treat from time to time," or else Friedrich and Beck would mechanically doff their hats, like foreign potentates going down a receiving line of well-wishers and admirers. They danced in a bar, and people came up to them who knew Sibylle, they were nondescript men, and all three of them united in despising them and played tricks on them, so for instance when one of them wanted to dance with Sibylle, then

Beck or Friedrich would stand up and fling himself into the arms of the man, as if that had been what was proposed, and waltzed the startled, hapless, desperate man away across the floor. Secretly, however, Friedrich and Beck never lost sight of each other. Each thought he was in with a sliver of a chance. They were no longer confederates. They were like men having to fight with daggers, but who still hadn't lost their respect, sympathy, and friendship for the other, and certainly they understood what it was that compelled him to thrust and job. They never left Sibylle's side. Friedrich's hands performed little ecstatic dances in the air. Their limbs were controlled by love. They were like wolves, baring their teeth, they had the smell of prey in their nostrils, but it was the law of their love that they would do nothing to harm the child. They walked her home. Their desire was not to quit her side, not to be cast out in the night; they craved to lie at the foot of her bed like dogs, that to them was bliss. But there was a light on in her room. It glimmered through the curtains into the night. "That'll be Walter," said Sibylle. "He's spying on me, so whatever happens from now on is his fault." Her expression darkened. Her voice grew harsh. She said: "You've got to come up with me now, we'll have a nightcap, it's early yet." Beck and Friedrich went along, thinking they were her protectors. To shield her from an attack of Walter's. Friedrich also with the intention of reassuring him about the childishly silly course of the evening.

Walter stood there, looking injured. He was hoarse. "We've got to talk," he said. He stressed the "we've."

"No, I can't, I've got friends here. I'm not so rude as you, not even saying 'good evening.' You're welcome to drink a schnapps with us, if you like."

"Sibylle!" That yell again. Naked and unprotected.

Something snapped in Sibylle: "I've had it, I've had it, I've had it, I'm not your creature, I'm not your slave, I'm not your dog, I can do what I want, and if you don't want to stand over me while I sleep with someone off the street, then you'd better get out and leave me alone." They were terrible words. Sibylle was in a towering rage.

Friedrich attempted to intercede. He said: "It was all perfectly innocent."

To which, facing Walter, she now added: "Yes, of course it was, of course it was harmless, but you're filth, everything around you is filth, and we're all drowning in it." Was it the cry of a girl who had been seduced? It was absurd and preposterous to think it was deliberate. But perhaps unconsciously? Was it a yearning for a condition that, by mistake, was gone and irretrievably gone? They were words that had the effect of opposing Friedrich to Walter, for whom in other ways he felt a lot of empathy. It was only some weeks later that he began to admire the critic who had found in this night of chaos the strength to free himself [but then Sibylle was never intended for him]. Walter spun off into a rage. Talked to her as though she was a common whore. Smashed tables and chairs and gramophone records, and played soccer with the books. Sibylle was laughing, laughing manically. The laughter spilled out of her like a torrent. Beck was laughing too. Friedrich joined in. The laughter was irresistible. Hell was ablaze. Walter slammed the door behind him and stormed down the stairs. It was the end of her relationship with Walter. She was free. Beck and Friedrich eyed each other. "Go, for God's sake, why don't you go?!" screamed Sibylle. She was crying. She fell to the floor sobbing. Beck and Friedrich sprang to help. "Go away, go away, take your hands off me, I hate you." And they went. For a while through the night together. A woman propositioned them, only to shrink back from their faces, which bore the rigid expressions of policemen. With a few polite and dignified words of their imaginary Russian, Friedrich and Beck bade one another good-night outside the stylish church that catered to the expensive shopping precinct.

There ensued a wild part of Sibylle's life. With the departure of the critic, her life had lost all direction. She acted in a film that wasn't even finished before the production company ran out of funds. She visited balls without enjoying herself, she knew a thousand people without thinking anything of any of them, she was a guest in many apartments without thinking she had a home anywhere. Friedrich and Beck were her friends. She went out with them, she cooked meals with them, she frolicked about in the woods outside the city with them. It would have been idyllic, had each boy not wanted the girl for himself. Finally, it was Beck [Sibylle was not intended for him] who left the trio. After enduring many humiliations, he found the ability to attach himself elsewhere. Friedrich stayed. Stayed with her. Close to her. At the foot of the bed in which she lay. He made her tea and soup when she was ill. He was in a desert in front of the cloud of a constant mirage. He was athirst for her lips. He was pale, battered, impecunious, hollow-cheeked, and desperate. But he fought on. Fought on with gritted teeth and fought, as he thought and continued to think, a fair fight. He refused to take her against her own will. He would lash out at anyone who used that word, "take." "She's not an object, she's a human being," he said. He would mount a passionate defense of her against all accusations. At such moments, his face would take on a calm and arrogant expression. "Oh, I can see you don't know Sibylle," he would say. The sentence was unwavering. There was no appeal to be made against it. There was no life belt that could be thrown to Friedrich. And then he resolved to die. "I can no longer exist without you." Sibylle was mute. What was she to say? An old line. Repeated ad infinitum since the dawn of humanity. "I can't live without you!" What a demand! What a claim! What a theft! Would he not be ashamed to say: "I can't live without your money, your watch, your ring?" Was she worth less than a watch or a ring? What a claim. "I can't live without you!" What a hopeless and helpless claim.

One evening, as Sibylle was still out with a man who had taken her to lunch, he went up to the north of the city to hook up with some figures in the criminal underworld. The fruit of his endeavors was a large heavy police revolver. It sat in his pocket like a weight. Friedrich had a natural sense of the ridiculousness of the situation. It was ridiculous running around, packing his revolver. The bullets that the dealer had shown him while loading the chambers would rip great holes in flesh and bone if the barrel was set point-blank against his chest. What a mess, thought Friedrich, what a horrible great mess. Then he had an idea. He would use the weapon to fight with, to bring the war to a conclusion with the most visible invest-ment of his physical being. He hurried round to Sibylle. Her win-dows were dark, the place was locked. He didn't have any money for a pay phone. The lack of ten pfennigs became crucial. "Ten pfennigs," he whimpered, "ten pfennigs." His happiness depended on having ten pfennigs. Doesn't the lover claim to be willing to do anything for the beloved? So Friedrich walked up to a man in the street. He said: "Ten pfennigs." The man was frightened. He jumped and ran off. Friedrich felt compelled: "I have to beg!" The idea that he might explain to someone calmly that just now, by silly mischance, he happened not to have ten pfennigs and that it was important didn't occur to him. The second time he went up to someone, he was shaking. His voice came out in an indistinct gurgle rather than a sentence. The second man looked annoyed. Disgust showed in his expression. He tossed a coin on the ground and hurried on his way. As Friedrich bent down to pick it up, he saw that it was a mark, and he was convulsed with horror as if by a high temperature. What use was a mark? He needed ten pfennigs. The machine would never swallow a mark. Machines are implacable. It's impossible to persuade them to depart from their normal course, even if it's to their advantage. Friedrich looked up at Sibylle's windows. He sent a piercing shout up into the air: "Sibylle! Sibylle!" Nothing stirred there, and it was only in the surrounding buildings that windows creaked and voices called for quiet. It wasn't till morning, when the people started to come out of their houses, that Friedrich quit his post. Where had Sibylle spent the night? Friedrich reeled, a wreck in the stream of the early traffic. He went to Beck's. At the foot of the bed, in which Beck was still asleep, he collapsed unconscious to the floor.

Beck felt compelled to have a word with Sibylle. He thought he was acting on Friedrich's behalf. He said: "He's going to do himself some mischief, I've seen the gun." He also said, since she didn't reply: "You've been with a few other men you've told me about, what is it that keeps you from going round to Friedrich's tonight and staying the night with him?"

Sibylle's expression remained veiled. "That's not the point," she said.

Friedrich caught up with her as she was on the point of shutting the elevator door. The conveyance took them up. Her lips trembled because of her proximity to him. He wanted to avoid all lugubriousness and give a cheerful sound to what he felt compelled to say. "You're smelling like a fairy again," he said as they walked into her room. "But do fairies have a smell? I prefer you." And he said: "Sibyllchen." She was doing her tiger pacing. The tension between them was unbearable. Sibylle said later that she was convinced that he'd come to shoot her. That was her interpretation of his taut pallor, though there was nothing more behind it than suicide. He started in to hack at the knot. He asked: "Can you name me anyone who loves you as passionately as I do?"

She said: "No," not raising her clear and beautiful voice, keeping it at a calm level, in the way she was to do throughout the whole confrontation. Her comportment was heroic. No heroine could have been braver. She was impeccable in her posture, and braced. Nor did she permit herself to be deflected into womanish blind alleys of argument. She confronted him. He admired her unreservedly.

"Fine," said Friedrich, and his voice and manner also remained calm. "I love you, you admit, the most of all the men who know you. I believe in this love of mine as an unalterable fact that has somehow been chosen to be my lot; certainly, I cannot be persuaded that it is a sort of idée fixe from the catalog of insanity. Now, what has happened with us, to my mind, is a misunderstanding. I need to sort it out, otherwise it will destroy me. People tell me you want to be taken. I find that remark as stupid as most of what people are pleased to spout in their mindless way. It's a bit of popular wisdom, and it doesn't impress me. If you were a girl whom I could beat and who would then kiss my hand afterward, I wouldn't think much of you. To me, you're a human being, and there is no triumphing over the dignity of another human being, viz. by destroying it. That sort of victory makes the victor merely despicable. It would be a victory that man celebrates over his own kind. But the misunderstanding between you and me, that misunderstanding is based upon the fact that you're a woman—and you don't want your body to be touched against your will, which may only be changed by touching you anyway, in spite of you. Maybe it sounds overintellectual to you. I have no choice. I am going to rape you. I will do so to clear our misunderstanding. But I will give your will every chance to assert itself, to meet force with force. Here is my revolver. It has six bullets. I will take off the safety catch and give it to you. You can defend yourself against my attack, and I ask that you do. If you shoot me, the law will be on your side, the moral law and the letter of the law. No one in the world will blame you or hold you culpable." He handed her the weapon. It sat like a cannon in her little hand. She made as if to weigh it. If only she'd shoot, thought Friedrich, if only she'd shoot. He was all ready to be hit by her. Death approached him in a surprising nimbus. Friedrich took a step forward. Then she raised the gun and fired. She was shooting at the mirror, in which they were both visible. The glass shattered. She fired one, two, three shots. Each bullet flew past Friedrich. Just past Friedrich. She has a very steady hand, he thought, and kept moving toward her. Then she threw the gun down.

He seized her; she didn't stir; he saw her face; it was calm, expressionless, averted; he felt her heart beat; she parted her pale lips just slightly, and said: "I don't want this." She said it without any emphasis. A little sadly. She had won. He let his arms fall. The tears started from her eyes. She cried, and he cried. They sat together crying and holding one another. They were disturbed by the sound of voices. The police were banging on the door, demanding an explanation. Friedrich had to go with them. A magistrate found him guilty of unlawful possession of a weapon, and of a breach of the peace. Then—was it really a mistake on the part of the official, or more a curious intervention of destiny in the course of events?— they forgot to take the gun off him, and Friedrich walked out with it still in his possession.

There was nothing for him but to leave the capital city where Sibylle was living. Beck had given him some money, and Friedrich felt he'd been deported. He spent some time in a monastery on an island in the Baltic. The spring gales tore across the sea. Friedrich sent telegrams until he didn't have a penny left for the official at the counter. The official took Friedrich for a madman. All the telegrams ever contained was the name "SIBYLLE! SIBYLLE! SIBYLLE!" It was Walter's cry, translated into the sober medium of post and telecommunications. Thereafter he yelled the name to the fields and waves. He plunged himself into work, followed the plow, made friends with the horses and cows. He told them about Sibylle. He talked about his love. The horses lowered their heads, the cows replied: "Moo"; they were a serious audience, and they were patient with him. A foal was born. No sooner could it stand than it showed affection. Friedrich named it Sibylle. He even kissed it on its fluffy pink muzzle. The mother made startled eyes and, after a pause for thought, expressed her approval of Friedrich's suit with a trusting scrape of her left hoof. Sibylle would go into Friedrich's room. She followed him over the fields and meadows and seashore. She would eat out of the hollow of his hand. Sibylle was gentle and affectionate, and grew to be a wonderful fox-colored mare, good and clever wherever she went. She presented the stallion to whom she was brought with an alert and clean-limbed foal like herself.

Days followed of fresh despair, which expressed itself in angry thoughts against the dear, good, innocent, and immaculate mare Sibylle. Was it right that he should have wasted so much time? Why had he consented to be banished; had he not simply fled? When he returned, after an interval of some months, to the capital, Sibylle was tanned from the summer, and a new scent drifted out of the little strips of rawsilk that were her dress and her shirt at once. They rode in a car throughout the city. She was radiant, a contented snail in an invisible house of joy; a young kitten rolled into a ball, feeling the pleasure of being itself, and purring songs of praise to the Almighty. She loved a man, and her love elevated her beauty into the pure concept "she is beautiful" that was beyond comprehension, and could only be venerated like the grace of genius whose presence abruptly is remarked in a sound from the throat of Orpheus, or a miracle of color, or the revelation of a poem. Their drive ended in front of a house on the green canal bank. "Come in," she said, and he made the acquaintance of an apartment full of old fittings, chests and cupboards and tables with broad surfaces that felt good to touch, and all the wood was richly carved, and on the walls there hung dark old paintings, dignified faces, and then there were weapons, sabers and pistols, and a knight's helmet; but that was from the last war. Bosporus met Friedrich with courtesy. Out of one of the old cupboards he brought bottles full of colored liqueurs, and he would only sit once Friedrich was seated, even though he was older, and dragged his wounded leg behind him a little. Bosporus was poor, but he had the ability with a gesture to create an aura of wealth about him. He also had the ability, in few, casual words, to draw a ring of mystery around his affairs. In the center of town, he ran a laboratory for chemical experiments; but the sign over the door bore a name that was not his; when Sibylle discovered this, the rumor started: he manufactures poison gas. Bosporus never said anything to the contrary. Did he know anything about Sibylle? He had taken her in. More could not be discovered. It was certain that he loved her, but what was just as certain was that he knew how to handle her. He listened to her young wishes and let it appear he didn't want to keep her. He was wise, and had the experience of danger behind him. The leash on which he held Sibylle was long and barely perceptible. Friedrich, who had a lot of sympathy and understanding for this particular case, still made the mistake of blaming himself. "It was a time she was all ready to love," he said to himself, "and I wasn't around." But Sibylle wasn't intended for Bosporus either. He was certain of that. He repeated, rephrased, the question he'd asked in the scene with the revolver: "Do you think Bosporus loves you more than I do?"

She said: "No." She even performed the tragedy of the woman unhappily in love, and with real tears. A touch of melancholy added further to her appeal. She was a good girl.

She often visited Friedrich. Spent whole days in his room, or he slipped back into the role of the runner, who raced panting through the city when he got her call. It was the time that Friedrich handed her over to the theater, sent her to drama school and had the happiness of rehearsing the ingenue roles of the classical repertoire with her. In the evenings, they would appear in public as a trio: Bosporus, Friedrich, Sibylle. Friedrich dressed the bride, she put on what he wanted, and she was led to Bosporus. People talked, Friedrich faced them down. "You're wrong," he said bluntly and decisively. "You're wrong. Sibylle isn't like any of the others. She's a goddess." His earnestness was invincible. Sibylle was the best-protected woman in the city. Friedrich's attitude would have been impeccable, if he hadn't still suffered from this terrible thirst. The thirst for her lips.

Then he became a beggar again, and stood in front of her and he was a damned soul without a body, and gasping and cramped, he said: "Your mouth, Sibylle, your mouth," and she forgot her laughter and took the happiness out of her expression, and said: "No, I like you." There it was once again, his devil in the guise of Sibylle, untouchable! Could you slap her if she was so calm and sensible and clever? His devil played at being her handmaiden. Friedrich served Sibylle. He helped her out of her bath, and rubbed her laughing with coarse towels till she was as red as a boiled lobster, a nice, sharp-scissored young lobster; but woe betide Friedrich if he should drop the coarse towels; woe betide him if his hands should settle on her skin, and stroke it in movements that were gentle, caressing, and full of love. A sudden transformation would occur, a metamorphosis in the adored figure, it was as if she pulled on, not a cap of invisibility, but a sort of magic shield that protected her from him from top to toe. "Leave," she would say, with chiseled features, and she was a statue of disappointment.

Then Friedrich would wander the thousand streets of the great city, through the day and into the night, wander blindly across the backdrop that all those who shared the time with him and the place, could see, and would hold judgment. He adjured God! [Never again would he be as believing as he was in his anguish over Sibylle, and it happened that he would go into churches and kneel down in front of the altars of saints, and pray to them for forgiveness and their blessing.] He showed himself to God as he panted and ran, in his perturbation and incomprehension, and he said: "Look, I fetch the wood for Bosporus's stove, I sweep the steps and lower my head, lest they see the welts and take fright at my rotting flesh, I would give my blood for Sibylle, I am all athirst for her mouth, oh, God, once only, a taste of those lips!" And God offered no reply while Friedrich cried His Name. It is perfectly possible that we have been sent signs and clues, but we overlook them in our zeal, with which we fail to advance our cause. And so Friedrich dreamed the dream of rapine. That dream too is as old as mankind, and Friedrich built a tower on a field miles away from human hearing and that offered no echo to any scream. And to it he dragged her [in his dream, oh, only in his dream] and set his demon in her guise, and fought with it and drove it out of Sibylle's body, and said: "Now stand condemned to howl and wail in this tower to the end of your days."

Still everything carried on. He served. Served Sibylle. Sure, he occasionally raised his weapon against himself, but what was a shot against the certainty, *She is destined for me*? Friedrich was not allowed to take himself off from this life that had Sibylle in it. "If she dies," he said, "then it's permitted." Did he desire her death? Who wouldn't like to see his demon destroyed? One night he woke up, and thought she had died. The thought was so ghastly that he hurried over to her, and sobbing, kissed her hands, while she wondered what had come over him. If life beside Sibylle was terrible, then it still had to be accepted in its terribleness, till the misunderstanding was resolved, the spell broken. And he even succeeded in breaking his dependency on her nearness, the habit of seeing her daily. He allowed her to depart on her first engagement, and he felt the train was passing over his own body as it left the station; but still he survived the test by thinking: She is in the world, she is breathing the same air.

ALL THAT was in the past. So had he perhaps come through the test, and was there an end in sight? He had better concentrate now—Friedrich stood up and stretched in the compartment, propped himself on his arms, morning had broken, sunlight spilled through the windows and a softer air—concentrate that he didn't make a mistake now, that the misunderstanding was not fealty to a love that lived solely off the strength of the past. Had he, during the months he hadn't seen Sibylle, distanced himself from her? Was it only her physical presence that beguiled him? Because in that case he was a fool, and it was his duty to break out of the madhouse of misunderstanding in his own emotional life, and leap into life, as long as there was a bit of happiness and joy to be caught. Had he not got through the night? Did he not overestimate the pain that he was in? Or was it that he was overly accustomed to the pain, and had therefore become immune to its deadly effect? He needed to account for his conduct. Perhaps he would have to write off those years with all their endeavor. Had he not traveled to the city in a bid to try and reach Sibylle after all, out of orneriness and in the guise of the man ostensibly passing through? *Sibylle, oh Sibylle!* Sunlight filled the frame of the window. And in the gleam of its light, Anja jumped down from her top bunk, and her body was all golden in the light. "Tuscany," she exclaimed. "It's Tuscany, and we're in Italy!"

They were in Italy. The south. The sun. There was the celebrated landscape of the Old Masters. In front of him, Anja still stood lustrously in the window. The breeze blew on her breasts. Shadow flecked the light on her skin. She stood there, enraptured: "Italy! Italy! Do you know why I had to come away with you? I wanted to go to Italy, I wanted to see Italy for myself. That was all that was driving me away from Magnus. This: the sun, the landscape, the green." It happened quite effortlessly, that they were drawn to one another by the sight. The rush of wind from a train going the other way threw her into his arms. In the cold whistling of a tunnel, he had to warm her nakedness. His kiss lit on her dry girlish lips; he didn't say "Little Anja," because he was thinking *Sibylle*; and since she clasped him to her, he steered their fall together on to the lower bunk.

They were in Rome, and Anja lived as she smoked, greedily and hurriedly, and she treated every hour as if it were the last [the prince's daughter who had seen Moscow burn, or some other town on the Volga] and tried to drain it of all its pleasure. Friedrich was astonished and amused. It was nice, it was simple, it was fun, girl-things lying around, and someone who said: "Sleep well," when night came, and in the morning, "Come on, the sun's shining," while two feet with little tidy toes were already kicking aside the blankets. But: "Am I that man?" he asked himself, as they curved out of the traffic-swarming *corso* across the Piazza Venezia into the Via del Impero, in a chariot drawn by a little horse. "Am I the man driving with a girl in my chariot past centuries of history towards the Colosseum, on my way to seeing the Baths of Antony behind the Palatine Hill?" Did the wonder climb out of the spectacular horizons ringing him, or did it fall on him with the beams of the sun, shining warmly in winter, or might it not be from anything that was happening to him, but rather the opposite, that he was acting, that he was taking steps forward or to the side, moving as though through thick forests when you feel You're going the wrong way, but for all that, and in spite of all your instinct, you're not able to follow the right path? He dreamed, but his dreams failed to make him happy. Nor was it a nightmare from which he awoke gasping. It was a dream of helplessness. The blurring, fuzzed images at the edge of reality. Did he love Anja? It was certainly pleasant not to be alone, but was it not also cowardly and reducing? There were times that he gave Anja money for the coachman, and leapt out of the carriage and lost himself in a tangle of little lanes. He visited the quarters of the poor, the gray huts on the banks of the Tiber. He wanted to be good, because he felt so bad. He bought fruit and dis-tributed it to the dirty, half-naked children. They are beautiful, he thought, under their crust of grime they are beautiful. He bent down to one boy and kissed cheeks that were plumped with the blood that had held aloft the power of the Caesars. He was sworn at, and he didn't understand. He saw a telegraph office, and he wrote the words: "I LOVE YOU, ONLY YOU, STILL AND ALWAYS," and he only understood that he had sent a wire to Sibylle when the words were already making their way down the wires to her. He followed soldiers and sailors into the shade of tight streets, supposing they were on their way to girls in brothels. He thought: I wish I were like them, working on a ship, and then going trustingly to find pleasure in a port. He had had enough of thinking. He distrusted it. He thought of Sibylle, Anja, Fedor, and Magnus, and he told himself: "I don't do anything but think about my desires. There's no truth there at all." He was a little dot in the vastness of the Eternal City. And even that, he thought, is overweening.

Anja couldn't do the taut and supple tiger walk of Sibylle, while she smoked and thought. She sat on the window seat in the hotel room with her soft mouth quickly, greedily sucking on her ciga-rette, dragging the smoke through her lungs and expelling it in short violent bursts into the air, looking at the Via Sallustiana and at the little church on the corner of the Via Piemonte. Draped in Friedrich's striped dressing gown, she was like a marmalade cat lying in the midday sun in sluggish contentment. She had made it, she was in Italy, the view of the street and the church completely satisfied her and gave her imagination a stage where she could per-form. Only her craving to lean against someone else, to feel the warm pulsing of another life next to hers, her skin's desire to be stroked by other hands, and the desire of her hands to stroke another skin, reminded Anja, when she was abandoned, of the absence of the tardy Friedrich. "Maybe the only reason we're together is because we haven't adopted a little dog, whose pretty little leaps would give us the illusion of being loved."

Friedrich sensed this the moment he walked into the room, and he thought: If I were alone, I would be confronted by myself and the emptiness around me, and I might do the right thing. He saw night approach like an enveloping fog. He was frightened by its predictable course. Once again, he would take his place beside Anja; the window would be open, and over their bed, the cool of the early spring night in Rome would waft like velvet, scented by early blossoms; again, they would listen to the shouts down in the street, all of them rising, as if sung, and the saber clink of the gendarmes on their rounds in their embroidered tailcoats of valets; once again, his mouth would find the mouth of the girl and taste the tobacco on her cool childlike lips; and once again, he would think of another girl and other lips [he was still athirst and in his desert, with his gaze fixed on an eternal fata morgana on the distant horizon]; all the while Anja, hurriedly and greedily and as if it were her last, sought to draw all possible pleasure from the mild hour. Were they not drowsing in a tepid bath, as old and tired already as Petronius, who, with his veins open, had put it all behind him? Friedrich then also buried his head in the sand, and, unable to flee from his own soul, conceived the error of leaving the place where unease troubled him. He wanted no more nights in Rome. He wanted no more soft beds. He wanted the excitement of journeying on, to a new place. "We're going," he said. "We're going farther south. Tonight."

IT WAS raining in Naples. They left the station, and thought they were in an aquarium. The carriage that they huddled in was as wet and cold as a boat on a windy sea. They swayed all down the length of the Corso Umberto. There was no one on the streets. They saw only strange figures that looked like billowing pantaloons in a storm, clinging to the black balloons of umbrellas. The tiles in the Piazza del Pretis were awash, you thought you were crossing a thin layer of melting ice over gaping marine chasms. At last their carriage trundled downhill toward the sea, and it took the sight of turbulent waves to remind them that they were on terra firma. For both of them, it was their first sight of the Mediterranean. They were disappointed and surprised, and they felt annoyed with themselves for being disappointed. The palms on the shore were trembling with cold. Vesuvius was a leaden cloud in the distance. Was this really Santa Lucia's city of sunshine? They stopped in front of a hotel on the Via Partenope and got out. We're about to run out of money, thought Friedrich. A tailcoat greeted them in soft crooning French: "*Messieurs dames* have brought bad weather with them, but it will soon pass. The hotel is at your disposal. You are my only guests, except for a Japanese consular attaché. He is waiting for a ship to take him home. It's still early in the year, the season has yet to begin. Are *messieurs dames* proposing to take a ship themselves?" His chatter contrived to be at once humble and mysterious. He seemed to want to say to them: "I'm afraid I am unable to offer you the warmth associated with Naples; I am inconsolable, but at least I can still offer you a Japanese diplomat by way of compensation." They took a room facing the Castel del Ovo; they opened the tall French windows to hear the pounding surf, the waves breaking against the walls of the old sea fortifications; and they turned on the central heating, to let the steam fill the pipes and warm them.

In the afternoon, Friedrich went into town by himself. Anja had built herself a nest of cushions in front of the radiator, and said she wanted to wait for the sun to come out. The rain had eased slightly, and with his coat collar turned up against the gale, Friedrich remained fairly dry as he crossed the Piazza del Plebiscito and onto the Via Roma, which was jam-packed with two streams of humanity, one preceding him, the other coming toward him, and over them was a buzz of voices like the wing beat of a great swarm of birds. Friedrich didn't mind that he knew no Italian and was unable to understand anything of what was being said. He had a sense of wildness, and an idea that everyone was on display: the young fellows in their smart suits and their olive green hats set aslant on their gleaming hair; the sailors in their short sweaters, their rolling stride, and their little mustaches; the officers jingling with their spurs and swords, under their cloaks worn dashingly over one shoulder; and also the women, their blue-painted eyelids demurely cast down, and their mouths a shocking red. His desire to have Sibylle with him grew frantic. Wouldn't it excite her? he thought to himself, and he saw her in love with the street, her eyes large and shining, and he could actually feel her laying her hand on his arm and saying: "Oh look at that woman over there, wouldn't you like to have her?" A tangle of little alleyways opened on the left. They were so narrow that if you opened your arms, you could touch the walls on either side with your fingertips. These too were full of people and bustle. Life was lived out on the streets. Wood fires had been lit in the doorways. The inhabitants assembled round a bonfire to which they had all contributed. The cold was damp and piercing. The smoke was acrid. It was the poverty of the south in wintertime. The stalls, however, were well supplied. Meats, cheeses, and breads: all were piled high on the tables. Fruit sellers yelled. Oranges were wastefully pressed and tossed to the ground, which they soon came to cover, like humus in the forest. This jungle is something you've got to see for yourself! His thoughts were still with Sibylle. He only responded to the new sights and sounds by imagining her delighted reaction. He endeavored to see through her eyes. He held long conversations with her, and he thought: This lane here is where I would kiss her! He quite forgot the hotel and Anja. He bought himself an end of salami and a piece of bread, and ate them up on his aimless wanderings. He went to a wine stall and had them pour him, from a dusty barrel, a glass of heavy red wine that tasted like ink. He bit into oranges, sucked out the juice, and, with the pleasure of oversupply, threw away the flesh. He saw a monkey sitting on a barrel organ and gave it a banana, which the monkey ate up in a rather well-bred fashion. Its master, who was cranking the handle, thanked him politely. Night had come, and Naples was lit by a thousand fires.

Then Friedrich emerged from the labyrinth of alleyways into the long rectangular Piazza Municipio, where a slight little man in a short raincoat, approached him, swinging an umbrella. "*Inglese, Francese, Tedesco*?" asked the little man, and said: "I direct you." The man was very wet and very cold. It seemed he must have spent the entire rainy day, from morning till evening, standing in the Piazza Municipio, waiting for a tourist. All the more determinedly did he now latch on to Friedrich, firing the speech that like a bullet in a gun had been inside him. The speech was leveled at Friedrich's body, so uncommonly small was the man, and it almost knocked him over. "Ah, he spikka Tcherman and he spikka all di odda langwitches. He wanna da help gentleman visita, who no understanda Napoli. He offer him girls, *Mädchen*, from Campagna, from Capri, cheap, vair cheap, but yong, no bad women, ah no, he have di addresses, only small fee fa da guide, *niente piu*, vair respectable, *e tutto compreso*." He swung his umbrella in the direction and set off after it. "We go," he said.

"No," said Friedrich, and grieved the little man by staying where he was. "Sorry," he said, "I don't feel like it. I'm sorry to disappoint you. But maybe you'll let me recompense you for having stood here waiting for me."

"Ah, no, no, no," retorted the little man, and made motions with his umbrella as though to take flight. "Signor no understanna nathin. Napoli! Is beautiful! Tarantella, da famous tarantella, genuine! Nude! Wi' two girls. Da signor watch. All positions! *Dieci positione! Dieci!*" In a gesture of utter self-sacrifice, the man let go his umbrella and waggled the fingers of both hands above his head, by way of demonstration.

You are a poor wretch, aren't you? thought Friedrich. Then why not go with the man and give him a sense of honest labor, instead of offending his self-worth by offering him charity? Friedrich dreaded the sights that awaited him. He could sense the thick gloom of a dirty bedroom with fly-spotted mirror and the shaming indignity of a show of maggoty pale flesh in a display of mechanical sex. He had never felt any curiosity about these things, and now, in his own upset, he felt he wouldn't be able to stand them. His own poor wretchedness stood revealed to him. Never had he felt so comprehensively hopeless. The city of Naples was a cloud that wanted to bear him away to some cloacal scrap heap. He could do nothing for the little man, and wanted to raise his arm in a farewell greeting to him and go, but the little man was trotting along beside him. But Friedrich was now taking the lead, and vaguely having his bearings, led them in the direction of his hotel.

"Oh," said the man, struggling with the wind, and trying to keep up, "oh, I understan', the signor not like women. I have served an English milord. I know antique naked Ganymedes. Like Museo Nazionale. *Dieci lire senza proviggione!*"

Friedrich thought: He's sweating now. He's afraid I may slip away, and he'll lose me. He's already lapsed into Italian. Then it occurred to Friedrich that he might take over the role of the tug, might cringe and wheedle and play a fiendish game with this man he couldn't shake off. "All right," said Friedrich, "ten lire it is. Now you come with me."

"No," the man was swinging his umbrella in passionate excitement, "no, there, there, we need to go there."

"No," said Friedrich, "I know where we're going, and we're going this way," and he stepped out even faster. Was this not the adventure of this city? Was this not a game that Sibylle would enjoy, that he could tell her about, suitably embellished, about how the desperate little fellow was jogging along, trying to keep up, and how they finally reached the hotel, and the little man stopped, and Friedrich took him by both hands and said: "No no, come on up, it's only ten lire," and in spite of his resistance pulled him, to the astonishment of the single hotel employee who had been dozing in the lobby, up the stairs to his room. This was the only adventure that Friedrich could have in Naples. He was playing "puss in the corner" again. He had always enjoyed that game. To Anja, sitting in the nest of cushions in front of the radiator, as if no time had passed at all, he said: "Guess what, I found someone in town who wants to see me in the guise of a classical statue of Ganymede, and is prepared to pay ten lire for the privilege!" He almost shouted it, and started rapidly taking his clothes off, in the manner of someone who is afraid he might miss a unique opportunity. The little man stood as straight as a guardsman against the door, and from the lowered standard of his umbrella, a little stream of water dribbled out on to the floor. "Take a seat, why don't you?" said Friedrich. "Make yourself at home. I'll dance the tarantella for you too, if you would like. Would you like it if the lady stripped as well? That will be another ten lire, I should tell you in advance."

The situation slowly dawned on Anja, who, at first hadn't understood what was happening. She perked up, like a rabbit with its nose quivering over a bunch of freshly plucked dandelion. "Ooh yes," she called out and jumped to her feet, "the gentleman is so nice, I'll only charge five lire. Five lire, special price," and already her hands were pulling at the cord of her dressing gown. Then the little man screamed. A shrill, piercing scream. A scream that cut to the bone, and blew away all the walls in the whole hotel. Then he hurled his umbrella at Friedrich, and ran out of the room. He crossed the corridor and flung open the door of the room opposite, as though to take shelter there. Standing framed in the doorway, under a bright pool of light stood a Japanese in a white kimono. In his hand, he was holding a scroll of paper and a short sword. His posture was that of an officer. He was evidently angry at the disturbance. The little man recoiled before the apparition of the Japanese as though he had hurtled into an invisible barrier, and he skidded on the linoleum floor, and lay there in the corridor.

Afterward, Friedrich never knew what he had thought in putting on this scene, or what he had intended to happen. He tried to explain it to the Japanese by saying: "I was acting on impulse. I wanted to find a victim I could sacrifice to my devil who had taken up residence in Sibylle." He picked the little man off the floor and gave him fifty lire. Friedrich wasn't a bad fellow. He had only seen himself so clearly in his poor wretchedness that when another poor wretch, his mirror image, had barked at him, he had to go and sink his teeth into him. In his heart he felt shame at being so poor and so small, but it wasn't the time to allow such a feeling to take hold of him. The Japanese still stood there in his white robe in the open doorway to his room. I gave him the cue for his entry, thought Friedrich, I must apologize for the disturbance I've caused him. He stepped into the other man's room and presented himself. He asked for forgiveness; he tried to explain; he felt driven to speak, to confess, to explain. The Japanese nodded. He listened. Polite, modest, outlandish only in his costume. He is a diplomat, Friedrich thought, and he said: "I can't be without Sibylle. Please understand, I can't." The Japanese inclined his wise head slightly. He understood Friedrich, he grasped the case, and he approved Friedrich's conclusion that he could no longer exist without Sibylle.

The man said: "I have prepared tea, for a night in which I want to stay awake." He walked over to a kettle that was humming over a light alcohol flame. He took it off the flame and put it down on the table. From a suitcase he took out three flat cups and put them next to the pot. Then he crossed into Friedrich's room and brought in Anja, who had stayed behind, leaning on the doorjamb, observing the activity with a soft, dreamy expression. He performed nothing really more than a single gesture, but it was irresistible. "This is the drink of my country," he said. "It is offered to new arrivals as a sign of welcome. Do me the honor of taking tea with me." And with a grave smile, he bowed—a measured, European bow to Friedrich; to Anja very nearly down to the ground—and it all struck Friedrich as incredibly oriental and Asiatic. They sat down and drank their green tea. It was hot, almost scalding, and they quickly felt its reinvigorating properties. "You are Russian," the Japanese said, turning to Anja, and he said a sentence to her in Russian.

Warmth came over Anja's face. "Oh," she said, and then some words, broken, groping, weighing them, in her mother tongue.

"It does her good," the Japanese said to Friedrich, thus apologizing for the conversation which he was unable to follow.

Perhaps Japan is what she yearns for now, thought Friedrich. If he tells Anja about his island and the strange and rare things on it, then she will belong to him. Anja has no home, there's only the country ahead of her that she can see. He saw her again as he had the first evening, in the foreign city. She can be so tender, he thought, and once again he had the feeling: You have to love her, like you would love an animal with soft fur. He thought it was perfectly natural that she would want to go to Japan, even though not a word had been said about it yet; and he was also pleased that she was to have the journey, the experience, the country, and the man; he wanted the best for her; it was probably all right if things between them ended in this fashion; and yet there was a little pang, a slight feeling of melancholy; she's leaving again.

"She is tired," said the Japanese. In other words, he wanted to discuss her transfer with Friedrich, as man to man.

They laid Anja on the bed, and her eyes rolled up under the lids as they came down. Friedrich thought: I am dealing with Magnus's property. His situation was making him act dishonorably. I always had contempt for those fathers, who, because they were beaten as children, go on to smack their own children. The man who was kicked, kicks out at others. Was it cowardly of him not to try and avert Magnus's loss? Then again, could he stand in Anja's way? By what right? How could he take a hand? Was that the law? Did he know what the law was? Was there a law that applied to them, to himself and to Anja, and Magnus, and the Japanese? He was no more cowardly than anyone else who was looking for the law and wasn't able to see it. Only he wasn't as crass as the most ignorant people, who, merely to accomplish something and to set themselves up in some way, pass decrees against their neighbors. Who is allowed to say: "You may not!"? Who dares to determine that for others?

The Japanese poured more tea for Friedrich and for himself. His hands were deft and quick, like the hands of a good surgeon. He said: "Why don't you kill yourself? I don't understand how you can continue to live. When, after listening to what you told me, I think of your sad affair, it seems to me that you are already dead, and leading a shadow life." The words were spoken with such immaculate courtesy that any objection to them could only have sounded boorish. "Do you know our idea of the honor of an officer?" he continued. "An officer may be unlucky and lose the battle, but if he's convinced he's done his best, then he cannot live with the error on the part of fate or—as you're a Christian—the misjudgment by God. What happened must be a mistake. He has suffered a stain that he did not deserve. He must look into the matter and correct it, there must be justice and process in the world, and, to remove the injustice, he kills himself. Or would you deny that you have lost a battle? Love and war are the oldest terrors. From them come unhappiness and chivalry; and while it may seem easier to be a victorious knight, think whether you, the loser, should not prefer to a miserable life the possibility of a knightly death? My words may perhaps sound strange and terrifying to you. I understand Europeans think differently. What prompts my speech is merely the circumstance that you came to me with your story just as I was wearing the white robes of an all-night vigil. This is a custom with my people. I am going home. Tomorrow my ship will dock from London, and in three weeks, we will land in Yokohama. During the voyage, I will wear the costume in which you see me now. I will draw up my reckoning with myself. I came to Europe to serve my country, and I have lost face. As you have. I too am in love. I too love a human being. I too love without luck and without hope. And I too say: 'She is destined for me; it is all a mistake!' But we are not so advanced in our philosophy and theology. I am going home to kill myself." His voice had not left its calm, precise, and quiet natural range, and the smile was still on his face. "Anja," he said, after a moment pointing to her, and his gesture was so infinitely polite and respectful that any objection would have been embarrassing and not to be contemplated, "Anja will come with me. She would like to see my country; she has said so; and I will show it to her. I still have that much time. And then I will send her back to Europe."

"But," said Friedrich, "as long as Sibylle's in the world, surely the misunderstanding between us can be cleared up!" The Japanese propped his wise head against his chest, and his eye traveled down Friedrich's body, down to his feet. That seemed to say whatever needed to be said, and he opposed Friedrich's hopeful counter with nothing further than his smile. Already Friedrich felt the cool brass doorknob in his hand, and when he looked across at Anja, the prince's daughter, asleep on the diplomat's bed, and her face lying in a valley in a range of white pillow hills, she seemed to have become a dreaming child again.

AND WHILE Friedrich was only left with the memory of soft features behind a veil of smoke and a recollection of tendernesses that were already like the desperate clutchings of a drowning woman around her would-be savior's neck, Sibylle, in her vision of Anja, saw a stronger manifestation altogether, a creature not unlike the medlar[3], gifted at exploiting its weakness, and in Anja's drifting in

[3] "Fruit of the medlar tree, resembling a small brown-skinned apple with a large cup-shaped eye between peristent calyx lobes. It is eaten only when decayed." (*OED*) The medlar—like the fig— has strong literary associations with the female sex, cf. Mercutio's lines in *Romeo and Juliet*, II, i:

> Now will he sit under a medlar tree,
> And with his mistress were that kind of fruit
> As maids call medlars, when they laugh alone.
> O Romeo! that she were, O! that she were
> An open *et cætera*, thou a poperin pear.

the swim of chance—from the day when still a babe in arms, she had seen Moscow in flames, or perhaps some other town on the Volga—she now saw the strangely purposeful steering of a wreck that had gone down, but not to the bottom, on an obstinate course that endangered all other shipping. Was she jealous, because Anja and Friedrich were traveling together? Sibylle was pretty sure she didn't love Friedrich. She loved Bosporus, but Friedrich was an object in her and no one else's possession that had newly got some color and had acquired visibility when it had left her orbit and, rejected by her, had removed itself with another party. Sibylle could see Friedrich and Anja strolling together in front of a body of water as blue as the sugar bags on the shelves of little corner grocery shops, under a sun of the lofty gold of a grandfather's fob watch. Meanwhile she herself was stuck in a perpetual shower-bath of gray rain. It was late evening, a public holiday. The houses were crammed with silence and inertia as with cotton wool. Even the barking of a dog outside a closed door had been reduced to a pathetic whimper. Sibylle hadn't left her room all day. She stood at her window, gazing down. There was no one on the street. It must have been fully an hour since the last person had stepped into the white pool around the streetlight.

Downstairs in the bar of the St. Peter's sat the members of the ensemble, which was not performing on that day, smoking and drinking at Magnus's expense. Fedor had asked Sibylle to come down. He had been quite blithe and cheerful. "It's going to be all right," he said. "Magnus will look after us. He knows Anja will only come back if we're here, so he can't let us fall." Sibylle had turned away. She had made a sacrifice and received no blessing in return.

What was it actually worth to her, the cabaret in the cellar of the Diana Variety Theater in the oldest street in the foreign city? On reflection, not a bean! The very thought of it disgusted her. It was a sort of abyss for somnambulists going to their doom. There are a few abysses like that in the world. In difficult times they are dug by people, who, acting apparently without self-interest, on a secret commission, dig a grave to give a particular burial to a few of the century's refugees. Sibylle took Friedrich's Roman telegram off the table and, not really reading it, held it in front of her eyes. The yellow piece of paper gradually came to rest, along with the hand holding it, against her side, and then joined her body in the swaying tiger stride.

FRIEDRICH HAD opened the tall French windows, and the curtains billowed into the room like lowered flags in the damp wind. Since leaving Anja in the Japanese man's room, he had felt freer than for some time. "I'm able to devote myself," he told himself, "unintermittently, and undistracted by anyone who's locked into the same four walls as me, to the thought of Sibylle." From his vantage point, the curving bay road was a line of lit lampposts, bending under the pressure of the heavy clouds. There were more lights over the sea, as it rolled up beyond the castle rock, against the harbor wall: red and green light signals and the sliding fire of lighthouses, revolving apathetically like clock hands on their unceasing patrol. Among the gray gunboats in the little military harbor, an occasional shrill metallic horn sounded its command. Every few minutes, a wave would tumble over the wall and drench the promenade in front of the hotel, where a new bay was in process of formation, giving off a smell of seaweed, fishes, shells, and salt, the universal coastline smell.

A man stood on the end of a jetty, watching a ship that was on the point of disappearing over the horizon. It was Friedrich, and at his back were the bright strip of sand of a northern beach, a brick tower, and the gabled houses of an old Hanseatic town. *Here and there alike, the waves chew the land.* On that night in Naples, the Mediterranean proved to Friedrich that it was no more than just another of the world's seas, its charms were merely generic, not charged with any particular revelations reserved for him, in the face of the old wonders. Friedrich found it resistible. It grew to be a matter of indifference to him compared with his love for Sibylle, and he felt a strong sense once again of the joy of being filled with a single desire. He was alone, and prepared to endure any pain. He believed the period of excesses was past, the period of errors and delusive consolations, and he was once more on the right way, which could only and always be the way to Sibylle. He had a ticket to take him to Sicily, but he had a mortal dread of that country that was still farther away from his beloved. How could he get to her in time, if she were lying somewhere ill? Before him he saw the temples of Agrigentum and the African sea, and it was a sight of such elemental scale and danger that just then, when he understood that he had not yet come through the battle of his life, he could not feel equal to it. The massy leaden plate of a storm moving up from Africa pressed the air over the mirror-smooth sea into a block of white-hot iron; the pillars of the temples turned ashen, and their cracked plaster crumbled away and struck the ground with the frightening echoey sound of drops squeezed from a loose tap into a basin; a man sat slumped on a mule, so swaddled in a blanket that he looked more like an amorphous bundle than a human being, carried by the patient beast through the hilly country, as the first lightning ripped open the gate of heaven. Friedrich was afraid of the lightning. He saw himself lying crushed beside the pillars. He didn't want to die; he mustn't die; he must go to Sibylle. The only possible salvation was the bell beside the door, and he gave the alarm signal. His finger stuck in terrible exhaustion in the dirty, ivory bell push, only relieved when Friedrich saw the face of the night porter before him in the crack of the door. He hurriedly negotiated the terms of his departure, and calm, the calm of the fugitive who has successfully managed the first stage of his flight over the barbed wire, came over him, and filled him with warm contentment as he sat in the carriage, listening to the easy trot of the horse, taking him through the deserted streets of the sleeping city to the nearest station. The hour he had to wait for the next train to Rome seemed never-ending.

SIBYLLE THREW a coat over her shoulders—it bulked up her slender frame—and strode out of the room. Her shining strawberry blond hair shone under the black beret she had pulled low over her eyes. Her face was troubled and pale, only the lips made a dark stain. She walked downstairs without switching on the light. The painted-over glass in the door to the bar was a little scratched, and through it Sibylle could see the members of the troupe sitting together at a long table. The lanky albino Magnus with his eyes of runny aquarelle blue sat at the end, in a tired posture of a man having to support his head on his hands to stay upright. The others were all laughing and talking. Fedor was preaching world revolution. His extravagant gestures made the world seem so small he could have tucked it under his arm and carried it off. That was what Sibylle got for her good deed. Nothing tied her to Fedor other than a desire—baffling to herself—to protect a naive and simple man. Suddenly she sensed what a calamity it can be to feel sympathy for someone else, and already she could feel the pressure of restraints settling round her like chains. Sibylle had ensured the continued existence of the cabaret and saved Fedor from being deported by sending the eager traveler Anja away with Friedrich; her calculation that Magnus would, in the teeth of all manner of official disapproval, step in to save the cabaret as the only possible point in the world to which Anja might one day return, had proved correct. Magnus had wanted to retire with Anja into respectable middle-class life as the director of a Diana Variety Theater of normal productions, only faintly and dimly associated—by the honorific management of the foundation that his father had established—with refugees. Now, however, through Anja's leaving, Magnus had become a true associate of all restless and unhappy people. Doctor Magnus, who had set up the old foundation for persecuted people, had, by the terms of his will, bequeathed his son and another, wilder age a dish of poisoned milk, a temptation around which a few wrigglesome snakes, one or two vipers, and numbers of gray mice had collected. In the face of this onrush of crafty, needy individuals, Magnus, the heir, was actually more helpless than they were, and felt more vilified than qualified. Vilified, for instance, by

A Sad Affair

Anja, who had come to him when still a little girl with whom he could have played catch, if he hadn't married her instead. His love for Anja had come out of a generalized pity for the poor waif, and the calculation this child will one day be a beauty. For her part, Anja had never seen him as much more than a sort of railway station with plenty of platforms, where one could wait with good prospects for trains to interesting places. The cabaret had been Anja's idea, and Magnus, as the more loving, and consequently, the inferior partner in his marriage, had been suitably supportive of it. And so a trench was dug, into which the wild and unstable enthusiasts, insufficiently drawn by the foundation for victims of persecution, fell as though shaken from a tree, irresistibly lured by the temptation of having found the proper stage for their ideas. At the time the cabaret was started, Sibylle had an engagement in the provinces, and found herself appalled at being slotted into the rigid hierarchy of an erstwhile court theater, at which approval to play Juliet might arrive roughly simultaneously with one's retirement.. At night she had wept in her respectable lodgings, and pummeled the pillows with her fists and cried for the time when actors had used to go around stealing clothes off washing lines, and no respectable family would have dreamed of letting out a bed to any actress. The straight lines and right angles of her provincial town were to Sibylle nothing better than the swept corridors of a prison between concrete walls. For the first time in her life, she had felt lonesome and abandoned. Friedrich had wanted to accompany her to the town, but she had turned him down because she had wanted to take Bosporus, who then hadn't come. His mysterious chemical enterprise that had got him (with Sibylle's help) the reputation for being

a wizard in poison gas, had suddenly and in rather a civilian fashion, failed, and, offended by the tormenting sensation I am poor, I
am her kept man, Bosporus, a hero and a knight, had withdrawn,
under an array of pretexts and pursued by creditors, to a regional
nursing home, where he had lived off his officer's pension. He had
brought his old weapons and his helmet along with him, and when
he walked, slightly limping, down the village street, then he was a
great man and a brave man. Sibylle, meanwhile, started writing
Friedrich long letters, and she would have liked to be able to call
him to her. However, her call would have sounded to him—who
saw her through love's eyes—like the call to a lover, and Sibylle
feared the arrival of one dazzled by happiness in a town where she
suffered nightmares of oversize traffic policemen. She loved
Bosporus; he was the angel in her life, he stood in the heavens with
a flaming sword, and from time to time she was overcome by the
thought: He was fighting for me! Friedrich had bowed to the
strength of this passion, he respected it with gritted teeth, even
though it was offered to a man for whom Sibylle was never
intended. Friedrich believed in her faithfulness to Bosporus. That,
to him, was a certainty that afforded him just enough tranquillity to
carry on with his life. Sibylle was not allowed to depart from that
faithfulness within sight of Friedrich. Or so she thought, and so,
instead of going to him, her unrest drove her to performances in
squalid nightclubs in the provincial town. The performances didn't
interest her. The songs croaked out of gluey mouths revolted her
with their beastly double entendres. She sat glum and bored over a
drink she didn't touch, and the eyes of the habitués around her, the
eyes that came with bellies, with short, stout thighs, the dissembled

traces of doubly beringed widowers' hands, slid over her almost without noticing. But it was her destiny, in one of these ovens of some middle-size provincial limbo, to see Fedor doing a turn there, a turn without the slightest success, yes, greeted even by vociferous disapproval. Since his appearance before such a hostile public [if they were expecting anything, they were expecting something crude, and mistook Fedor for a revolutionary] took on something of the sudden pause of a breathless runner, he reminded Sibylle of Friedrich's most pitiable condition, as he reached her bed breathless after a long run. She felt aghast and compassionate, and, after having Fedor brought to her by a waiter, was surprised to find a human being who looked thoroughly poor and abject, and yet behaved with complete insouciance. He dismissed his hostile reception with a contemptuous reference to "stupid provincial bigwigs" and, after first making sure that his colleague from the legitimate theater was paying, filled up his glass. Sibylle was uncertain; she still had Friedrich somewhere in mind, she feared complications, and took Fedor's manner for that of a man who kept his cards close to his vest. Not until later did she realize that what you saw was what you got, and she was overcome by a protectiveness for a simple child who wanted to stay with her. That feeling, and her desire to get away from the bureaucratic atmosphere of the erstwhile court theater to a more chaotic stage that would look automatically more artistic, prompted Sibylle to run away with Fedor from the provincial town and go to the basement cabaret in the oldest alley in the foreign city. But she was too aware not to realize quite quickly that the scruffy colorful path of bohemia was only going to lead to the same barren and unsatisfying work as the calm and sober road of a more officially sanctioned career. Then, only the excitement of an unspecified curiosity held her. The Russians were strange. Magnus was strange. Performing in the twilight basement was strange. Cabaret was something she had snuffled at as the mouse snuffles at the bacon rind in the mousetrap. And now she was trapped, caught up in it, in conditions and events that were as remote from her as court intrigues in Manchuria, and—well, was she still that Sibylle who would have opposed almost to the death any restriction placed on her freedom?

She turned away from the painted glass barroom door to the front door. She opened it, and at the same instant, the wind leapt violently into the corridor. Sibylle heard a shout, and she ran out into the street; not until she saw that no one was coming after her, and it was just the door falling shut behind her, did she walk on more slowly.

FRIEDRICH CLIMBED into a third-class carriage on a train that had come up from Reggio, on the southernmost point on the peninsula, and was caked with soot from the many tunnels going through Calabria. The handles on doors and windows were grimy, and an acrid paste coated the hands of the passengers who had hauled themselves aloft, and from there, via involuntary gestures of impatience, their faces, which bore dark streaks so that they resembled half-finished masks. The inside of the carriage looked like a homeless shelter. The passengers, who already had a long journey behind them, lay variously sprawled or hunched on benches, floor, and rows of suitcases. In the cool blue glow of a night-light, it was at first not easy to separate one figure from another in the tangle of arms and legs and heads. The sleepers were a single many-headed and many-limbed organism. Friedrich was afraid he might stumble and fall, and he was further irritated by the sounds of breathing all around him in every pitch. He had a feeling of having broken into some strangers' bedroom, and he was relieved when he finally found a place on the end of a bench, not far from the door. After his eyes had gotten used to the space and the light, he saw that he had joined a group of young people, who were all wearing different parts of the same naval uniform. They were recruits, narrow-shouldered boys, who had been drafted into the navy, and were on their way to join their units. Four of them were sitting opposite Friedrich, and three on the bench beside him, so that he restored symmetry and equilibrium to the benches. Each young fellow had his knees spread, touching his neighbor's, and together their upper thighs made a bed of supple, taut muscle on which a girl was laid sleeping, while the faces of the youths who were on their way to serve, and who resisted the girl because of the natural need for sleep in the young, and dreamed through the night with open eyes, their skin transparent and lit as though by inner fire in the exhaustion of the late vigil, constituted a kind of heaven above the girl's sleep, noble and full of the beauty of the south. No queen could enjoy a better and better-protected sleep, and never will you be better loved, thought Friedrich, struck by the chaste manner of the group, to which he, a stranger, had somehow come to belong. He guessed that this girl, whom they permitted to sleep through the night thus bedded, was the girlfriend of one of these boys, whom out of love and passion she was seeing to his ship, and that the others, out of friendship for him, were all devoted to her and in love with her. The girl was beautiful. His feeling more than his senses told Friedrich she was. Love transfigured her. She lay in a holy aura. She was beloved and in love, and she was a pleasing thing in the natural order of the world. Was she not a child in a cradle, over whom the men were reverently bowing their heads? And how submissive they all were to the beautiful law of love. Surely they all desired the girl, but they left her to the one with whom she was affianced, instead of proceeding against him in a common violence of fists and murder, to tear her away from him and anyone else. They did not suffer. They laid other features on the face of the sleeping girl, and thought of their own girls slumbering, at night. Friedrich warmed to them. He brushed the arm of his neighbor, and he wished for a few moments he could be like that again, simple and in a state of grace and escaped from his destiny. But then, as the train drew near to Rome, and the first gardens became visible in the early light, he too saw the image of Sibylle in the face of the sleeper, and in an enormous desire he bent down into the line of lowered heads of the young sailors. Then the girl awoke, and they all saw themselves in her eyes, and they were glad, glad for no reason, and all embraced one another, and laughed and joked.

SIBYLLE HAD walked down to the end of the road, and then turned in the direction of the lake. She went the same way she had gone with Friedrich, when he had visited the foreign city. The streets were quiet and deserted. Occasionally a car would pass or a pedestrian would come up the other way, his coat collar turned up

A Sad Affair

and walking with long, hasty strides. If she heard silence behind her, then she knew that he had stopped to watch her, until, despairing at her continued walk, he would turn and carry on. Sibylle reached the lakeside road. There was a pause in the rain, and from behind a cloud a piece of the moon peeped out to illuminate the loose and broken cloudscape. The wind too had settled, and the lake was a smooth, black mirror. Like ink, Sibylle thought. The lights of the facing shore had lost their haze, and now each one burned separately, and projected its own clear, personal reflection on the surface of the water. A last streetcar crossed the wide bridge. The squeak of its wheels could be heard long after it was gone. The two conductors stood alone together in the brightly lit carriage. Sibylle went to the hotel where Friedrich had stayed. She rang the bell for the porter, and then ran away and hid behind a tree when she heard the approach of firm steps and a jingling of keys. The light over the door came on, and a man stepped out on to a little area under a roof that covered the drive. He stood as on a stage, a scarf around his neck, the keys in his hand, and looked around crossly. He shouted something that sounded like an oath and went back inside. The light went out at the same moment that the moon was masked by a cloud, and it was as though it too had been extinguished by the irate porter. For a while there was total darkness. Only gradually were the outlines of things reestablished in the light of the streetlamps. Sibylle was annoyed with herself for not asking for Friedrich. She knew he couldn't be there. But she would have liked to have asked the question, and heard an answer to it. There seemed to be some point in that. The air wrapped itself around her like a damp cloth. Everything returned: the rain, the wind. It was like a cold compress laid around the chest of someone sick with a fever. The patient shivers and grimaces, and the red, cracked hands of the nurse strike him as incredibly cruel. Sibylle walked down the steps to the quayside, and wandered along the water's edge, stumbling over gravel, rubble, and dirt. She walked there because she was afraid. She walked there because shudders ran down her spine, and because she saw masked murderers in every shadow. Was she not the Sibylle who was sufficiently free and courageous to follow the prompting of any moment? Was she a prisoner in her room at the Saint Peter's Hostel, a slave to the cabaret, the mistress of Fedor, who would be waiting for her with his simple soul's irritating cheerfulness? She picked up a stone and chucked it in the water. It sounded as if the lake had gulped and had to force it down. Sibylle threw more stones. She listened to the sounds they made. "The lake's gurgling, it's gurgling!" she cried. When she'd stood here with Friedrich, she had had the feeling he had wanted to glide into the deep with her. What if someone came along now, who would simply push her into the water? Would she scream? She was already screaming! Shrilly, in a demented treble. She felt the touch of hands on her, and didn't know they were her own. Was she condemned to be the victim of some man? She herself had wanted to be like a man in the way she chose a lover, and gave desire and responsibility the slip. Was that it, that she wanted to avoid the fate of the woman, and, more actively and more intellectually obsessed than other girls, to play the knight herself, the one who comes and confers grace and happiness as the mood takes him? Had she not selected and used up the men who were her lovers? Had she not been the one to speak to Bosporus and court him, once she was excited by his veteran's limp? Had she not resisted Friedrich because she refused to give in to the demands that were implicit in his love? And had she not taken Fedor to herself because he was nothing more to her than an animal in need of shelter that had lain down in front of her door one night? Sibylle walked on. The moon peered out of a window in the clouds again, and pinned a long shadow on her, reaching down to the water. Her fear calmed. She was out of terror's clutches. She looked around for a flight of stairs up to the lakeside road. All at once, she stopped and laughed. A wild, child-like laugh. She wondered which of the men she knew would understand her night walk. She pictured their horror, their astonishment, their surprise, the words: "You must be mad!" and almost burst with laughter. Only Friedrich would understand her walk. No one else. She knew that. When she reached the road, she trotted glumly home, like a schoolgirl weighed down with the many unsolved problems in the satchel on her back.

IN ROME, Friedrich was praying. He knelt on the flags at the shrine of a saint whose name he didn't know. Friedrich had had a Protestant baptism and upbringing, and he wasn't at home in a Catholic church, but never had he prayed with such fervor. The cathedrals he knew were bare, lofty barns, without any swirl of incense. White unadorned pillars stood in rigid lines supporting the beams. The roses of their capitals flowered invisibly. Here, though, God and His saints were on view, and you could raise up your voice to them, and complain and accuse, and pray for a blessing. Like most men of his age, Friedrich had led a churchless life and not felt any deprivation. Nor did his kneeling in Rome betoken any sort of conversion. It was a surge of desire, belief, and hope that broke from him, set in motion by the sight of the group of young sailors and their chaste darling with whom Friedrich had traveled. In the station, he had bought wine and offered it to them, who were going farther, to Livorno. They had duly passed the bottle round among themselves, from mouth to mouth, and to the mouth of the girl, and raised it before drinking and said: "Here's to your beloved, Signore!" And when they went away waving and laughing, Friedrich thought once more: I wish I were like them. And then he had sent off a couple of telegrams. One to Sibylle with a twenty-word reply paid for. It told of Friedrich's separation from Anja, and asked Sibylle to tell him if he might see her, or if she wanted to meet him somewhere. The return address he gave as a hotel in Bologna, whose name he had once heard. The other telegram was sent to a place from where Friedrich had hopes of being sent money. Then he went straight on to Bologna, and that had been the extent of his second sojourn in Rome.

TIRED OUT after her walk, Sibylle had thrown herself down on her bed. Her coat hung down to the floor, while she lay on its sleeve and collar. She hadn't undressed further. She was relieved that Fedor hadn't been waiting in her room, and that, in fact, his window was dark and he seemed to have gone to sleep. Sibylle remained awake. She waited for a bell to sound. Surely news would come for her. It was the pauper's wait for the postman. You hear him set his foot on the bottom step, he's on his way up, perhaps he's bringing news, a message that'll provide a ray of hope or a meal for that particular day—when he turns on his heel, just before the crack of our door, turns back, and we hear the quick taps of his iron-heeled shoes as he scuttles down the stairs. Sibylle's bed was a raft on a boggy pool. She heard the gurgle all round her of hollow bubbly sounds, and the wizened faces of ancient toads emerged out of the muck and stared at her with mightily bulbous eyes. She didn't want to set foot on the cabaret stage again. She didn't want to see Magnus again, or Fedor, or any of them. She remembered the dressing-room reek of rancid fat, strong perfume, soap, sweat, and alcohol, and it made her feel sick. She felt like screaming again, but she didn't want to show her fear, her dread, to anyone, and it might have brought out Fedor, which would have been insufferable to her at that moment. Outwardly, she would have to continue to be the secure, brave, and sensible Sibylle. The raft mustn't capsize. The bog mustn't wash over her. There was no one to help her, not Bosporus and not Friedrich. And there was no news.

Outside, it was getting light. Firm strides tramped along the pavements outside. The workers were leaving their homes and going to their factories. A streetcar screeched to a sudden halt. Sibylle could feel in her teeth the grind of the jammed wheels on the smooth rails. Her room looked cool and bare. She looked at her stuffed toys, her bears and dogs and donkeys, and thought they still looked asleep. Then she got out of bed, went up to the mirror, and saw that she was still the young Sibylle with the delicate features. Her wakeful night hadn't caused her face to slacken. The skin was taut with a tension that looked well on her. Her eyes had a swimmy sheen that might have come from the kingdom of dreams. Sibylle made herself ready with a care she hadn't shown for a long time. She dealt with a profusion of waters, lotions, powders, and essences, made a careful choice of underwear, dress, stockings, and shoes, and was as beautiful, clean, and fragrant as any young English lady paying her first call on the Queen, and then, with a quiet cry, she threw herself back on the bed to await the ringing of the bell.

IN BOLOGNA Friedrich was standing in the "Two Towers," in an old smoke-blackened room, in front of an ancient stooped man, who, with trembling, almost tearful voice, was saying: "Yes, there is post for the gentleman, yes, there is post there, if I might see his passport, yes, of course, very good, sir, there is some post," and he passed Friedrich a telegram. Friedrich had to go over to the window to be able to make out the writing. The shadows of the two towers leaned heavily down on the old inn. When he looked out of the window at the masonry, he couldn't see to the top of them. Two endless, crooked paths seemed to be leading up to heaven. When they collapse, they'll squash us, thought Friedrich. He was afraid to open the telegram. What sort of rejection would Sibylle be shouting to him this time?

SIBYLLE HAD come charging toward the boy who had brought Friedrich's second telegram from Rome, and had thrown her arms around him, because a message spelled the way out for her. The jaws of the trap loosened, and the grille slid aside leaving a chink she could slip through. She threw everything she had into a large suitcase, sat down on it, and got the lid shut. A whistle, a shrill, gut-tersnipe-style whistle out the open window might be sufficient. A taxi would drive up, the driver would pick up the suitcase; she was free, she could get away from the bog. But: Was that what she wanted? Was it necessary to flee? Did she have to sneak away unnoticed? Could she not cut the ribbon of camaraderie, of an empathy that was foreign to her and that she hated, openly and in front of everyone? She lapsed into the tiger stride. She crisscrossed the room. The grille was shut again. She had shut it herself. But now she was a dangerous wild animal, with teeth and claws. She knocked on Fedor's door. Her face bore the veiled expression that Friedrich had got to see so many times. "I'm leaving." Her voice was harsh. Fedor rolled over in bed, and asked what the weather was like. He hadn't understood her. Sibylle was sorry she had come. Was it still flight, if she left him asleep? She said: "Afraid it's rain-ing," and she slammed the door behind her.

FRIEDRICH KEPT rereading the text of the telegram. Was it not a fanfare, a jubilation, an annunciation? "MEET ME VENICE," it said. "MEET ME VENICE TOMORROW MORNING," and it gave an exact time as well. Was that not a miracle? Friedrich went out onto the square. He saw pigeons grazing in front of a church. The pigeons of Venice, he thought. He owed thanks to God, his prayers had been answered, a miracle had befallen, Sibylle was coming to him, he would see her, hold her in his arms, hand her into a gondola; he had better set off for Venice right away. The heavens were lofty and bright above the two towers. Friedrich hurried back into the inn.

He felt he owed the old man an apology, because he was going on without having slept there. He ordered some of the old man's best wine. In the shadowy bar, it looked as black as elderberry juice. Friedrich invited his host to drink with him. He said: "Sibylle." The old man loudly clacked his tongue. A slow and heavy heat came from the wine.

It was night by the time Friedrich reached Venice. He was there to choose Sibylle's billet, and he didn't know where to turn. The station platform was like a building site. In front of a half-built wall were troughs of mortar and large white cement sacks, some of which, overfilled, had burst, and spilled their dusty contents across the platform so that your shoes went white as you walked. Then a passageway lined with faded posters took in the travelers, only to spit them out in front of a serried row of hotel agents. Friedrich didn't dare to succumb to their chanted appeals or to the famous names on the brass badges on their caps. His money was almost gone. Unless he was sent more—I must send another wire, he thought—and with Sibylle, he would spend the last of his lire in a week at the outside. That calculation irked him. He felt like a debt-laden wastrel. Why hadn't he been more prudent, and saved up his money for Sibylle? He cursed his trip with Anja and her expenses, in a way that was unattractive and wasn't really him. The hotel agents, who hadn't managed to fish any guests out of this last train of the day, moved grumpily onto the waiting platform for the vaporetto and shoved Friedrich out on deck with them. He stood by the rail, heard the signal for departure, saw the pistons begin to move, and sniffed the hot steam smell of the boiler. A cool breeze blew down from the bows. From the greenish canal water, a line of white foam rose on either side with a soft hiss. The frontages of the buildings could not be seen in any detail. From time to time you could make out some gaudy landing poles in front of a palazzo. The dark entrances of lateral canals were sinisterly silent. After they had passed under the arch of the Rialto Bridge, Friedrich got out. He followed his yen to be somewhere in the heart of the city, and he booked a couple of rooms for himself and Sibylle in a simple hotel close to the vaporetto stop. They were inexpensive, and one was over the other. Friedrich moved into the downstairs room so as to be able to hear Sibylle's footfall above him. He put himself to bed with the desire to hear that footfall.

He barely slept, and was up early. When he pushed back the shutters, he was suddenly flooded with light and noise. The sun stood over the canal. The white arch of the bridge seemed to float in its flittering light. The gondoliers loomed over the bows of their vessels. Friedrich went out into the throng of the market behind the bridge. He bought fruit and flowers, and dashed back to the hotel to decorate Sibylle's room. He put the flowers in various containers, and pulled a couple of books out of his suitcase. The ride to the station was a ride through sunshine and past meridional ghosts. The dead seemed to peer from every window of every palazzo—they had built Venice, and now they couldn't tear themselves away from their labor. They were behind every pillar and in every ray of light. They had to endure a great chill in a later epoch, and they were wicked conveyancers to all the pleasures and deaths of their time. "This is where you shall love," they cried, and the traveler desired to love there. "This is where you shall die," they cried on another occasion, and the traveler desired to die there. How would

Friedrich be able to stand it if Sibylle failed to show? That too was possible. Friedrich looked up at the station clock, feeling so tense with expectation that he sought to push the hands toward the time of the train's arrival.

Fear of missing Sibylle on the platform had led Friedrich to take up a position behind the barrier, in front of the serried hotel agents. The travelers pushed past him in a black stream that he scanned with impatience. There was no Sibylle. The stream dwindled, dried up, the porters returned empty-handed to their bench in the waiting room. Had Sibylle really not come? Was his fear realized? And his crushing disappointment? Friedrich wrestled with the machine that dispensed platform tickets. He charged through the barrier, and veered toward the platform. A ribbon of gray stone lay between the brown ballasted troughs of the rails. Friedrich was breathless; his eyes flicked over the stone to the end. There was a suitcase, and a person. It was Sibylle. She was waiting. She was standing next to her suitcase, her coat draped over her shoulders in military style, and waiting. A ray of light fell through a gap in the grimy glass roof of the station and lit her face in such a way that it looked like a picture thrown on a screen by the conical dust beam of a projector in the cinema's artificial night. Friedrich stopped running barely two steps from where she stood. Sibylle laughed, and Friedrich laughed. All at once, they were overcome by an embarrassment that was so great that, without a word, they picked up her suitcase together, and wandered off to the exit. Not until he was calling for a gondola did Friedrich use his voice.

They rode in the gondola, and both of them perceived it as a coffin, as they glided along the little canals with their hands on the black, lacquered wood. They sat side by side like the lovers of a thousand descriptions, and they both perceived it at the same time, and they both separately started for the other seats in the middle and upset the balance of their craft, which began to wobble violently. They looked at one another as they laughed. Once again, Friedrich attempted to fathom what was going on behind the smooth oval of her forehead [oh, how he would have liked to place his hand over it]. He knew nothing of the torment of her last days in the foreign city, but he sensed: She is all alone in the world now. In her face exhaustion from her train journey mingled with the excitement of having arrived and the stimulus of the new place. Might he not cover it with his kisses—it was more alabaster pale than the faces of the young sailors on the train to Rome—the brow, the eyes, the mouth? He watched her lie stretched out on the floor of the gondola, and he was bent over her, breathing in her breath, and he wished the journey would never end.

The flowers in her room were a further reason to look away. Was he expecting thanks? Sibylle was angry because he indicated through signs what she already knew. "I would have come even if you hadn't called me," she said, and then she regretted having said it. She saw the shadows settle round Friedrich's eyes. She saw him striving to keep an expression of friendly equanimity on his face.

"See that bridge?" he said. "That's Shylock's bridge." Why did he say that? Who cared? Was it his way of luring her over to the window, to have them both looking out onto the canal, so that he could be cheek to cheek with her, and feel her hair, without them having to look at each other?

They made small talk. They exchanged observations. Sibylle filled her lungs, became alert and radiant; she was taking to Venice. They walked through the alleys, stood on bridges and squares, in cool courtyards, they felt the beauty of smooth pillars, ate in small tucked-away restaurants overlooking the small canals, drank strong black coffee in the sumptuous hall in St. Mark's Square, and, where their imaginations were fired by a masked ball, they were tempted to dance. Days they spent in this way. In the mornings, they played at getting lost. They plunged out of the hotel into the tangle of serpentine alleyways, and tried to keep going in the same direction. They passed through lanes and courtyards that were so narrow that their shoulders brushed against the damp masonry on either side. Then Sibylle would walk in front of him. Seen from behind, she was a boy. He loved having her near enough to touch. After wandering for hours, they sometimes reached the edge of the city. The ground fell away steeply. Ahead of them was the lagoon. It was a visible frontier. Beyond, an abstract geometrical rectangle, was the cemetery island. Gondolas ferried the coffins across from the mainland. The steamer wailed a warning that did not interrupt the sleep of the dead.

Gradually, Friedrich and Sibylle came to hate Venice. If they were to avoid the assault, the horrible nakedness of its ending, then there was only the piazza with its cafés, its tourists, its brazen waiters, postcard sellers, and tour groups outside the garish fairground of St. Mark's. Sibylle took against the pigeons, referring to them as "overfed gluttons." She favored the cats. She would go up to them wherever she saw them, and told them of a campaign they should mount one morning, all the cats of the city together, to storm the piazza in an almighty phalanx and eat up the pigeons. Friedrich would sometimes go into the church, while Sibylle stayed outside and returned the glances of the officers—who would ceremonially carry their polished sabers in front of them in black or blue or gray cloth—with such calm, seriousness, openness, and frank appraisal as to confuse and terrify these cavaliers. Friedrich no longer prayed. Full of revulsion, he watched the tourists fill the nave with their field glasses and cameras. He turned to look at the choir. In their low seats sat old men—white, crumpled ancients with red caps on their bald heads—mumbling their litanies. They too were among the dead of this city. Could they help him? The place was infected by the chill of dead hearts. The patterned tile floor had been worn concave by the knees of innumerable worshipers who had long since departed this life.

Once, they crossed the lagoon to the Lido. They rented bicycles and bowled along the promenade behind the beach and the bathing huts. Sibylle seemed to float on the shiny metal. She flew in front of him, and he gave chase. He would catch up, but then she would craftily give him the slip once more. They tumbled breathless onto the sand, in the midst of a group of bathers who, in spite of the early season, had already ventured out. They were a mixed company of young people, playing gramophone records in the sun, and they extended a jolly welcome to Friedrich and Sibylle. The pleasant wistfulness of English dance tunes seemed especially thin and delicate against the beat of the waves. The boys and girls danced together on a wooden pier. They laid their brown arms round their hips, in stark contrast to the white of the bathing suits. The girls pressed themselves against the boys. Sometimes one would throw her long arms around her friend's neck, while he spun her round in a circle, till she dropped on the sand with a breathless squeal. Friedrich and Sibylle had the same thought. Why could they not join in? They didn't dare hold hands, they knew it was an impossibility. They leaped up, as though they'd seen a ghost, and without saying good-bye, hurriedly pedaled off.

The past was brushed over. They didn't talk about it. Sibylle didn't mention Fedor or Magnus, the cabaret or the foreign city. Friedrich didn't mention Anja. They tried to exist like two people who happened to have run into each other in Venice. There was a wall of glass between them. It was only in the evenings that it sometimes became a little thinner. Then they would go upstairs, laughing about the hotel manager who, in unctuous front-of-house fashion welcomed Sibylle with an "I kiss your hand, Madame." The manager liked Friedrich and Sibylle. He treated them with the respect that two young people deserve, [he was touched by them] who, for the sake of appearances, he thought, and out of nervousness, rent two rooms instead of just the one. Each time he bade them good-night, it was with benevolence and irony. He would have liked to spread his arms over them in benediction like a priest. Sibylle was laughing herself silly. Friedrich laughed as well. But in his heart he wasn't laughing. Bedtime followed a long-established routine between them. Sibylle was shown up to bed. Once she was under the blankets, in her realm, it was forbidden to sit on the bed. Friedrich had to draw up a chair, and read her a fairy tale. "Another one," she would say when it was over. "Another one, please, I want another one," and she reached out her hands imploringly, and he wasn't allowed to seize them. They were always the same fairy tales. Sibylle had heard them when she was little. She lay there and dreamed. Friedrich had already devised a technique that permitted him to read the story and gaze at Sibylle at the same time. Her face was never lovelier than in these dreamy hours before sleep. Friedrich loved that hour, loved reading aloud, and loved the fairy tales, because he loved Sibylle. He read her to sleep. After the third fairy tale, she would be away. Her breath had fallen into the lovely easy rhythm of her nights. Her nose pointed to him; her mouth pouted, and between her lips there was a shimmer of white teeth. He watched her breathe. Her throat rose and fell. Her blood pulsed. Nothing in the world to Friedrich was as lovely or desirable as Sibylle's face asleep. For seconds at a time, though, when the thirst for her lips overcame him, he would hate her; but her sleep was sacred. Was it not in his keeping? Friedrich was afraid Sibylle might wake if her lips felt the touch of his. He was afraid of her scream. Her horror that would wash over him. Above all, he feared betrayal. Only after hours spent watching did he leave her room, feeling utterly reduced.

His room was below. It was the identical room. His bed was below her bed. He knew when he lay on it that he was directly underneath her. Why did God not answer his prayers? His body burned in the sheets. The bed was in flames. He was a man on a spit. Gone out of her room, out of her sleep, he damned himself for not being a beast. He talked nonsense. He yelled up at the ceiling. It remained immovably gray white. Had Sibylle not come to him? Had she not been sent to him? She was destined for him, wasn't she? But, because she had come instead of being seized, she enjoyed the protection of the laws of hospitality. He came up with these antique notions, at which the whole planet would have laughed. His devil in her guise had come to call.

Sibylle awoke. Was that the door? Was someone in the room

with her? She thought she heard footsteps and the sound of someone breathing by her bed. Was it Friedrich? Sibylle didn't dare put
out her hand; she was afraid of the dark, dangerous space over the
bedclothes, where it might be seized by unseen hands. Did she
want any confirmation of that? She lay there, listening. There was
nothing to be heard. She knew: Friedrich is in his room downstairs.
She knew: He is lying under me, unable to sleep, and his love is trying to drill through the ceiling and the floorboards. She knew: He
is on fire. The blood fled from her lips; they grew pale; the blood
shrank back into the heart. She felt her face turn chill. A river of ice
crept under the blankets; it flowed over her throat, across her
breasts and belly, and she felt it moving further down, covering her
skin with little goosebumps and freezing her thighs. What if she
went to Friedrich now? The thought mustn't be spoken out loud.
She pressed her lips together so hard that her mouth was like a
dam. The teeth bit into her flesh, and she tasted the salty, teary
taste of blood, and felt a brief, thin stream trickle down her chin.
I'd sooner let my blood flow than scream! She had a sense of bright
blood. She would have liked to look at herself in a mirror, to study
her face, to scrutinize its every pleat and fold, all its planes and ele-
vations, but her arm didn't trust itself to go on the short journey
from its cave under the bedclothes to the switch of the little lamp
on the bedside table. Sibylle saw she had made a mistake. The mistake was to have come here. But whom else could she have turned
to, if not to Friedrich? She thought about Bosporus, and knew that
she could only have gone to Friedrich. She missed him when he
was far from her. He was the person who belonged to her. Did she
love him after all? No, no, no, she did not! But when she wasn't

forced to see: He loves me, he's suffering [even though she needed the feeling that Friedrich loved her], perhaps she loved him then. "I see him looking at me, and it kills him," she said to herself, and then she hated him. Was it her fault that he loved her? Did she intentionally cause him to desire her? Once again, she wished she could have a mirror and light. Like all young women, she sometimes had a dreadful feeling that she was growing old and ugly. She knew that on the day Friedrich failed to notice her, on that day she would be old. She longed for him to come; she was sorry now that there was no one in the room; but she also thought: If he does come, he'll look at me, and I won't be able to stand being looked at. Why wasn't she an animal, a bird, a cat, a small dog, just some animal that he liked? In those nights, she thought she could have slept with any man off the street, only not with Friedrich. She thought: There will be another great Flood, and everyone will die; only Friedrich and I will be spared. And she saw two figures pursuing one another. They ran after each other shouting, on a green, blue, and brown globe that spun round on an axis, just like the globe in geography class at school.

After such nights, they were both tetchy and irritable. Since each was expecting an attack from the other, they both reacted oversensitively, like delicate instruments, to every sound they thought they heard. Their speech became coarse and aggressive.

"Stop staring at me," cried Sibylle. "Take your hand off me!"

"Who would want to stare at you," Friedrich shouted back, and he spluttered over the sarcastic laugh he tried to produce.

Sibylle was writing a letter to Bosporus: "It's impossible for me to stand Friedrich any longer. It's just impossible."

Friedrich took the letter to post it. While she'd been writing it, Sibylle had worn her inscrutable expression. Did this letter contain the thoughts behind her brow? Did Friedrich at last have her thoughts in his hand? He saw himself in a mirror in a barber's shop, and he blushed. He hated the squalid and petty transgressions of curiosity, little landlady nosiness about the post of her lodgers. Friedrich had caught himself out. He despised himself. His red face looked swollen. The flesh round his eyes was all puffy. He went right up to the mirror. He asked himself: "How can anyone love me?" He inspected his hair. The people all around didn't bother him in the least. He lifted strands of it. Was it thinning already? Was he making a mess of his life by clinging so desperately to Sibylle? He was twenty-seven. The blood left his face again. It was thin and pale and no longer puffy. He walked on, and saw Sibylle's face like a white mask in front of him. What if she'd set down her secret and written out the wish that might animate the mask? Was the letter he was holding in his hand the thought behind her brow? Friedrich tugged at the paper. Perhaps he was seeing ghosts, perhaps his eye was deceived, perhaps she did love him after all and was merely caught up in some obstacle? Of course, she loved him, the misunderstanding must be set aside; Friedrich opened the envelope, and the letter lay open before his eyes under the green shade of the post office lamp: "It's impossible for me to stand Friedrich any longer. It's just impossible."

"She must die. She must die." He whispered the sentence to himself, in the way that simpleminded old people play the same thought over and over again. What was he guilty of? What had he done, what had he done to her? Didn't he do everything for her?

Didn't he live for her? Would he not give up his life for her? He clutched the counter. A man eyed him, curiously, inquiringly—maybe a doctor, maybe a plainclothes policeman. Friedrich let go of the counter. It sailed away from him. He staggered in a vast emptiness. The man supported him. "No!" said Friedrich. "I just need an envelope." He pulled a white envelope out of a dispenser, and, not disguising his handwriting, wrote out Bosporus's name and address. Then he put Sibylle's letter in the envelope, stuck it and stamped it and dropped it in the box.

At the counter for *poste restante*, he asked if some money had arrived for him. The official shook his head. "*Niente*," he said, "*niente*," continuing mechanically to sort letters into various files. Friedrich was on the street again, buying four large children's balloons from a vendor. One was blue, another green, the third was red, and the fourth yellow. Also, he bought fruit and some peeled almonds, because he knew Sibylle liked those.

She was happy, smiling, beaming, nibbling. Friedrich tied the balloons to Sibylle's bedposts. They hung in the room's still air like four moons. The almonds crunched behind Sibylle's lips, and he could smell their sweet fragrance. *It's impossible for me to stand Friedrich any longer. It's just impossible.* The lines felt as though they had been crammed down his throat. He felt full of them. His heart struggled to beat past them.

"What's the matter?" asked Sibylle.

"Nothing," he replied, "nothing," and he tried hard to imitate the indifferent expression of the postal employee automatically sorting mail.

He was quite certain: I don't hate her. He didn't curse her; he cursed the sinister powers of dark forces. Where was the transgression? What was he being punished for? "I love you! I love you!" he said suddenly. He screamed it to her. She sat on a chair, and looked up at him.

They had spent all the money they had, and didn't have a penny left for food; all the houses suddenly put their kitchens on show and sent sizzling sounds out into the streets, and spicy aromas. The sun covered St. Mark's Square, and the bells on a hundred clock towers chimed noon. Sibylle and Friedrich covered long and pointless distances. Friedrich drilled his toe into the stone slabs of the square. He was choked with shame and rage, and he felt like digging his way into the earth. Was Sibylle hungry? He felt as though his skin was pierced by thousands of needles. The pigeons hovered just over their heads in a dense swarm. A man in a cap scattered corn for them. The camera shutters clicked and clacked. Sibylle and Friedrich didn't say a word. They looked coolly off into the distance, like superior people who take their meals late, and like to stroll to work up an appetite.

And as they walked, it happened—after a long time, and they were standing before the lagoon facing the Lido—that the silence between them had grown so huge that it filled the canopy of the sky quite to bursting. And then Friedrich said: "Little Sibylle." And he stopped at the foot of a bridge and saw the water of a canal flowing into the lagoon, and he saw how young and beautiful she was, a fine, courtly figure on the quay next to the water's edge, a line of shadow in the bright air that was worth more to him than any and all air, and he took her and held her in his arms and kissed her, in the full bustle of the roadway, full on the mouth. He tasted something he couldn't quite place, it brushed his lips, he inhaled its fleeting fragrance, an aroma of almonds and sea air, and it was happiness. He looked into Sibylle's face. It was so near that he could feel the fluff of invisible little hairs on her skin, but so far that he could see it entire, round and full. It was perfect. A face without any flaw. Her eyes were open wide, her gaze calm and fixed. He felt her life. He held it wrapped in his arms. He could lift her up into the light. It all took a fraction of a second, and he was flooded with the miraculous.

I have touched her mouth; I have kissed Sibylle. He sprang up the steps; he hopped across the bridge on one leg; he limped down the other side, and he did many things for Sibylle's amusement.

They took a different way back, stopping in front of every shop window of the commercial street. "Would you like it, the material, the bracelet, the silk scarf, the Nile-smelling handbag of crocodile leather? I'll give it to you. I'll give it all to you!" Sibylle nodded. His gestures were magnificent. He spread all the treasures of the world at her feet.

In the hotel, there was a telegram waiting for Friedrich. It instructed him to go to Ragusa on a certain assignment, and to that end, gave him credit with an Italian bank. "You can go home. You can go back to Bosporus, if you want. You can look for a new engagement. You will play Juliet." He held her hand. Her face was sparkling in so much light. She lowered her eyes, and he kissed her eyelids.

She nodded. She thought for a moment: I could go with him; and she saw herself lying stretched out flat on the white, sand-scrubbed deck of a boat, looking up at the clouds wafting gently overhead. There was a lot of light in her hair as well. It was as though firelight was playing across her. She nodded. "I'll go home. I'll play Juliet." They both laughed, and they knew nothing had changed, and that the wall of glass was still between them, sheer as air and acutely reflecting the image of the other. It was a frontier that they now respected. Sibylle remained destined for him; Friedrich was the human being who belonged to her. Nothing had changed.

ABOUT THE AUTHOR

WOLFGANG KOEPPEN, the illegitimate son of a doctor who took no interest in his welfare, was born in 1906 in Greifswald on the Baltic coast. He was a student for a time, unemployed, and held an array of odd jobs including ship's cook, factory worker, and cinema usher. At the same time, he began to write for left-wing papers and by 1931 was in Berlin, writing for the *Berliner Börsen-Courier*. *Eine unglückliche Liebe (A Sad Affair)* (1934) was his first novel, published with the Jewish publisher Bruno Cassirer, followed by *Die Mauer schwankt* (The tottering wall) (1935). Following the publication of these two works, he emigrated to Holland for a short period in the mid-1930s. Prior to the war, he returned to Germany and spent the war years writing film scripts for UFA that were, as he put it, just good enough to keep him in work, and just bad enough not to be made. The end of the war saw him in Munich.

In 1948, he ghostwrote Jakob Littner's Holocaust memoir *Aufzeichnungen aus eniem Erdloch* (Notes from a hole in the ground), for which he was paid in food parcels. In 1992, the book was somewhat controversially republished under Koeppen's own name. The controversy was renewed when Littner's original manuscript, having been traced and translated into English by his relative, Kurt Grübler, appeared as *Journey through the Night*, published by Continuum in 2000. Critics have vindicated Koeppen, analyzing

Littner's original text next to both Koeppen's and Grübler's versions. Ruth Franklin, writing in *The New Republic*, demonstrated that Koeppen remained quite true to the original and in no way betrayed the truth of Littner's account.

In the 1950s, Koeppen completed the three novels that established him, alongside Günter Grass and Heinrich Böll, among the leading contemporary German writers: *Tauben im Gras* (*Pigeons on the Grass*) (1951), *Das Treibhaus* (*The Hothouse*) (1953), and *Der Tod in Rom* (*Death in Rome*) (1954). Although quite separate in terms of character, action, and setting, these three novels, taken together, comprise a kind of trilogy on the state of postwar Germany. German readers and reviewers, however, were wholly unequal to them, taking particular umbrage with *The Hothouse*, which suggested that ex-Nazis, now acting as politicians in the Bundestag, had merely changed their spots. Pilloried by the critics, Koeppen, either too proud, or too lazy, wrote no more fiction thereafter.

For the remaining forty-odd years of his life, he was a sort of literary pensioner kept by Suhrkamp, his loyal publisher, and by a series of prizes and awards that, guiltily and belatedly, came his way, among them the Büchner Prize of 1962. He wrote three travel books, on Russia, America, and France, and a memoir, *Jugend* (Youth), that appeared in 1976, yet he never wrote the new novel that was touted and promised over several decades. In 1986, Suhrkamp published his collected works, somewhat surprisingly running to six volumes. He died in 1996, shortly before his ninetieth birthday. In the summer of 2000, a 700-page collection of *inédits* was brought out under the title *Auf dem Phantasieroß* (On the wings of imagination).

After the American and English publications of *The Hothouse* in 2001, there has been a renaissance of interest in Koeppen's work. "German writers knew Koeppen as an essential bridge," wrote the

Wall Street Journal, "as the first postwar voice to speak of things as they are." Nadine Gordimer described it as "lyrically inescapable. . . . Scathingly beautiful in the nightmare landscapes of the failure of materialism's Supermarket to assuage the human inner destructions of the past." And Ruth Franklin (in *The New Republic*) declared, "It is hard to think of a German writer of his generation who has written more sensitively or more profoundly about the Holocaust and its effects than Wolfgang Koeppen."